# The Curse of the

# Mummy's Case

*Volume 5 of the*

*Case Books of Octavius Bear*

## Harry DeMaio

*"Alternative Universe Mysteries for Adult Animal Lovers"*

Paperback ISBN  978-1-78092-770-1
ePub ISBN  978-1-78092-771-8
PDF ISBN  978-1-78092-772-5

Published in the UK by MX Publishing
335 Princess Park Manor, Royal Drive,
London, N11 3GX
www.mxpublishing.co.uk

**Dedicated to GTP**

**A Most Extraordinary Bear**

**and to the late**

**Bob Gibson**

**A Graphics Genius**

# Acknowledgements

These books have evolved over a long period of time and under a wide range of influences and circumstances. I am indebted to many people for helping to bring Octavius and his cohorts to the printed page. Thanks most especially to my wife, Virginia, for her insights and clever suggestions as well as her unfailing enthusiasm for the project and patience with its author. To my sons, Mark and Andrew and their spouses, Cindy and Lorraine, for helping make these tomes more readable and audience friendly. To Cathy Hartnett, cheerleader-extraordinaire for her eagerness to see this alternate universe take form. To Jack Magan, Rick Talerico, Dan Andriacco Amy Thomas, Luke Kuhns and Zohreh Zand for their assistance and support.

Kudos to Jim Effler, Brian Belanger and the late Bob Gibson for their illustrations and covers. Thanks, of course, to Steve Emecz and MX publishing for giving Octavius et al. a great home.

If, in spite of all this help, some errors or inconsistencies have crept through, the buck stops here. Needless to say, all of the characters, situations, and narratives are original and fictional.

# Also from Harry DeMaio

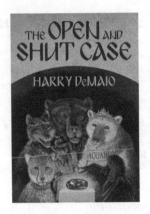 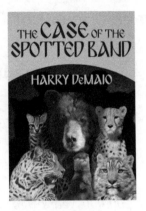

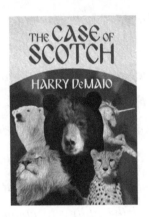 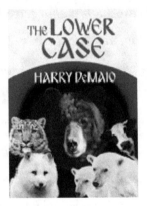

The Open and Shut Case

The Case of the Spotted Band

The Case of Scotch

The Lower Case

# The Development of Civilization Volume 5 Part 1

## <u>Our Origins</u>

### *(From "An Introduction to Faunapology" by Octavius Bear PhD.)*

*About 100,000 years ago, according to scientific experts, a colossal solar flare blasted out from our Sun, creating gigantic magnetic storms here on Earth. These highly charged electrical tempests caused startling physical and psychological imbalances in the then population of our world. The complete nervous systems of some species were totally destroyed. For example, "Homo Sapiens" lost all mental and motor capabilities and rapidly became extinct. Less developed species exposed to the radiation were affected differently. Four-footed and finned mammals, birds and reptiles suddenly found themselves capable of complex thought, enhanced emotions, self-awareness, social consciousness and the ability to communicate, sometimes orally, sometimes telepathically, often both. Both speech production and speech perception slowly progressed with the evolution of tongues, lips, vocal cords and enhanced ear to brain connections. Many species developed opposable digits, fingers or claws, further accelerating civilized progress. Some others (most fish and underground dwellers) were shielded from the radiation and remained only as sentient as they were before the blast. This event is referred to as **The Big Shock**. It remains under intensive study.*

# The Players in Volume 5

**Octavius Bear** – Mega-sized Kodiak; Narcoleptic war hero; Consulting Detective; Scientist; Inventor; Seeker of justice; Mega-billionaire owner of Universal Ursine Industries; Gourmet/gourmand; Somewhat sedentary and grouchy just on general principles.

**Mauritius (Maury) Meerkat** – Narrator; Assistant to Octavius; Theatrical Agent; African *émigré* with a French-Dutch background; clever with a shady history.

**Bearoness Belinda Béarnaise Bruin Bear** *(nee Black)* – Gorgeous polar superstar, with the Aquashow, "Some Like It Cold." Now wife of Octavius; Extremely rich widow of Bearon Byron Bruin living in Polar Paradise in the Shetlands; Owner-pilot of the last flying Concorde SST.

**Arabella Bear** – Hybrid bear cub prodigy; Twin daughter of Bearoness Belinda and Octavius.

**McTavish Bear** – Hybrid bear cub prodigy; Twin son of Bearoness Belinda and Octavius Bear

**Inspector Bruce Wallaroo** – Irrepressible but brilliant marsupial; an international law and order genius from Down Under; often calls on Octavius and Maury for support.

**Otto the Magnificent** – **AKA Hairy Otter** - An absolutely terrible illusionist magician, Otto the Magnificent escaped the claws of the evil genius Imperius Drake, but not before he developed some amazing powers courtesy of Imperius' genetic alterations.

**Frau Schuylkill** – Octavius' beautiful Swiss she-wolf housekeeper/cook/pilot/security officer with many other mysterious and military talents. She rescued Octavius from his dive off the Breakurbach Falls while he was struggling with his nemesis, Imperius Drake.

**Wyatt Where** – Another wolf. Former military intelligence officer who had retired to a security post at the Bank of Lake Michigan in Chicago and then quit to join Octavius.

**Howard Watt** – Porcupine. High tech security authority who also left the bank with Wyatt Where to join Octavius. A laser and particle beam accelerator expert.

**Benedict and Galatea Tigris** – White Bengals. The Flying Tigers

**Chita** – Beautiful, fascinating, clever, sexy, immoral and highly independent feline who among other things, is the publisher and editor in chief of *PURR* and *SOW* magazines.

**Uraeus – (Raamjet) -** Egyptian Cobra; demi goddess; protector of the tomb, coffin and mummy of King Tsk VI.

**King Tsk VI** – Hippopotamus. Cruel and vicious Ancient Egyptian king; Leader of the Languishing Leonine Legions (Lions) and the Pharaoh's Phalanx (Crocodiles)

**Imperius Drake** – "Moriarty with wings." Arch-villain, leader of the Black Quack gang; brilliant but loony duck who has developed a serum to make the animal kingdom his slaves; seeks world conquest and vengeance for ridicule by the scientific community and the death of his beloved mate, **Lee-Li-Li.**

**Bigg Baboon** – The major muscle in the Black Quack gang; the archetypical dumb heavy.

**Effendi** – An Egyptian vulture – arranger of events and relationships, mostly criminal.

**Hyena** – An Egyptian low-life who is also an expert on hieroglyphs and tomb robbery.

**Bearyl and Bearnice Blanc** – Belinda's stunning twin polar sidekicks; Actress and singer, respectively.

**L. Condor** – Andean Condor cyber-net genius with a 12-foot wingspan.

**Leperello – (Lepi)** Himalayan Snow Leopard and singing partner of Bearnice Blanc.

**Mlle Woof** – Bichon Frisé; Governess to the twin cubs

**Mrs. McRadish** – Sheep - Cook at Polar Paradise / Bearmoral Castle

**Fiona** – Dandy Dinmont -Manager of the Polar Paradise cocktail lounge

**Dolly, Molly, Polly and Holly** – Cloned sheep Maids at Polar Paradise / Bearmoral Castle

**Dougal** – Shetland Sheep Dog – Major Domo at Polar Paradise / Bearmoral Castle

**Superintendent Nigel Wardlaw of Shetland Yard** – Bearded Collie –The Scottish Police.

**Major Akil** – Egyptian Mau (cat); head of the Egyptian Antiquities Police

8

**Hamid** – Egyptian Pharaoh Hound – driver and expert on Saharan trails

**Farouk** – A Red Sea fishercat

**Kemal** – a camel and sole owner and proprietor of *Ships of the Desert Transport.*

**Fetlock Holmes** – The Great Horse Detective and sometime associate of Octavius Bear.

**Juno Bear** - Octavius' mother and twins' grandmother.

**Agrippa Bear** – Octavius' half brother.

**Doctor "Odd" Vark** – Aardvark – Chief Geneticist at Universal Ursine Industries.

**Doctor Chiti BingBang** – Orangutan – Chief Physician at Universal Ursine Industries.


## Locations in Volume 5

Cincinnati, Ohio; Polar Paradise / Bearmoral Castle, in the Shetlands; Sites around Egypt

# Prologue

## *Somewhere in Egypt*

*Far, far below in the fetid gloom,*
*Carefully moving from room to room.*
*She's a thief on the run*
*But big trouble's begun.*
*She is facing her moment of doom.*

They were coming. She could sense them more than see or hear them, but they were there and they were moving fast...faster than she could move. The crudely dug passageways were dark. There's dark and there's DARK. And then there was this - REALLY DARK!! She was hoping she wouldn't run into anything slimy on the floors or hanging from the ceiling as she groped her way along the walls, lugging a burlap bag filled with her latest "acquisitions" – a golden flail, crook and battle crown from the burial room of the predynastic God-King Ka Rek. She had a flashlight but didn't dare turn it on. They were too close.

She thought it had been too easy. Now she knew why. It was a trap! And like a stupid chump, she fell for it. The map! The half-excavated tunnel! The false doors, the arcane hieroglyphs promising great rewards to the courageous, the daring! They should have mentioned "the greedy." They've been trying to get her for years and she had always evaded them. This time might be different. There were no little side passages or caverns where she could hide. Just the rough walls of the tunnel.

She was working her way upward. That much she could be sure of. But upward to what? When that ceiling fell in behind her, cutting off her return route, she was left with no alternative than to pass through the burial room. After digging herself out with her bare hands, she had heaved against a stone door and fell through into what felt like a series of connected chambers and then into the tunnel she was stumbling along now.

Where was she? Why are these tunnels here? Perhaps the priests had assembled in these secret chambers and then magically appeared before the royal family and courtiers who had gathered to pay their last respects to the earthly manifestation of the god-king. Illusions, always illusions!

She hoped this was another passageway leading all the way out. Of course, the priests could have just gotten down to the mummy room before the others and simply waited. But that didn't sound like any priests she'd heard of. They'd want to be sure no one saw them before they made their mystical arrival, probably with smoke, mirrors and chiming bells. No, she thought, more hopeful than sure, this had to be an alternate entry (and exit) system for the tomb.

Whoever was following her knew the passages well. Occasionally, she could actually see them or at least, see the flickering light of their torches as they appeared and disappeared in the intersecting tunnels. She could vaguely hear the "thump, thump" of their feet. Or was that her heart? All she could smell was the fetid air that had managed to survive inside the tomb over the millennia. She was trying to be soundless but it wasn't easy. Every now and again, the contents of her bag would clatter as she moved or ran into something. She should have brought some cloths to deaden the sound. Not like her to be so unprepared but this one had come up suddenly and she couldn't resist. Now she'd probably pay for her recklessness.

Wait! She heard a rustling sound dead ahead. Were they coming for her from both directions? She couldn't figure out how they had gotten past the collapsed ceiling behind her. All the more reason to believe it was a trap.

She stopped. She looked behind her. Nothing for the moment, although she thought she heard footsteps. But up in front, that rustling sound again. Should she risk the flashlight? No choice!  She switched it on and saw a vague, shadowy outline on the floor about twenty feet in front of her. Two red lights glowed at her. Steady, intense, like LED's. Some kind of alarm sensor? In a four thousand year old tomb?  C'mon! She turned off the flashlight. The red lights remained glowing. Well, they weren't a reflection. That rustling sound again from the direction of the lights. They were moving. Toward her!!! The tunnel at this point was arrow-straight both ahead and behind. No place to hide. She placed the bag against the wall, drew out her gun and checked her assault knife. Whatever it was kept on coming. Should she turn on the torch again? Why not?

She did and the red lights stopped moving for a moment. But now it didn't matter. She could see it clearly. The "lights" were the glowing eyes of the largest cobra she could ever imagine. Fiery eyes; golden scales; crested head erect; mouth open; deadly fangs prominently displayed and forked tongue flicking in and out. The thing was at least ten feet long. It had stopped moving forward and began to coil again. The rustling sound! Now accompanied by sporadic "hisses."  Its coils blocked the passage ahead. This was a Uraeus, a cobra sacred to the gods and sent by them to protect the king and his belongings – in this world or the next.

12

What to do? Should she take her chances on shooting the snake before it spit venom at her? Cobras didn't have to bite to kill and they were deadly up to a range of eight feet *(if her course in early Egyptian herpetology was reliable)* and right now she was too close. On the other hand, there were the fast closing pursuers, number unknown, but intentions certainly clear.

From behind her a voice rang out: "Arabella, shut down your video game console!  McTavish, you too! It's time for bed!"

"Awww!! I'm winning!"

"You are not!!"

The voice again: "This minute and no arguments!"

She turned to her twin brother cub and growled, "You cheated. Where did you get that snake?"

**"What snake?"**

Octavius

# Chapter One

## *Polar Paradise / Bearmoral Castle*

*We're back in the land of Scottish frost.*
*All hope of warmth is completely lost.*
*I'm a meerkat, you see.*
*Ice is wasted on me.*
*I'm searching for heat and at any cost.*

Welcome to the Shetlands – super chilly setting of *Polar Paradise*, or if you are more traditionally oriented, *Bearmoral Castle*, home of Bearoness Belinda Béarnaise Bruin Bear *(nee Black)* and her mate, Octavius Bear. A few explanations are in order before we go hurtling off on our next thrill-packed adventure.

First, let me introduce myself and a few other players. My name is Maury (Mauritius) Meerkat, also known as Your Genial Narrator; African Meerkat; Octavius' indispensable assistant; operative; scribe; overall facilitator as well as a pretty clever detective, if I do say so myself. I am also a part time theatrical agent for several lutrine and ursine talents we will meet shortly.

Octavius Bear is a huge Kodiak – over nine feet tall and 1400 pounds. As you may also know, among his many talents and accomplishments, he is a brilliant, self-taught practitioner in the wide ranging fields of biology, physics, ursinology, voodoo, teleology, chemistry, apiculture and oenology. He is a self made gazillionaire and sole owner of UUI *(Universal Ursine Industries)* as well as a first rate electrical, electronic, structural, marine, aeronautical, mechanical and chemical engineer. The Great Bear has a few other interesting

15

characteristics such as falling into brief, deep narcoleptic comas – side effects of his successful genetic experiments to eliminate the need for him to hibernate. Like many of his species, he is also given to emotional outbursts.

However, the talent and occupation that should interest you most is his avocation for criminology. The Bear works in close concert with Inspector Bruce Wallaroo from Australia, of whom more later, and with his own Cincinnati based team:

- Frau Ilse Schuylkill – Swiss she-wolf; security officer; housekeeper-cook; jet pilot and sharpshooter with many other strange and arcane abilities.

- Colonel Wyatt Where – another wolf; ex-military hero; security specialist and pilot; Frau Schuylkill's equally bizarre mate.

- Doctor Howard Watt – porcupine; brilliant scientist and technologist; laser and weapons specialist. Now leading the Multiverse project.

- Senhor L. Condor – Andean Condor cyber-net genius with a 12-foot wingspan and artificial voices.

- Otto the Magnificent – AKA Hairy Otter – An absolutely terrible illusionist magician, Otto the Magnificent escaped the claws of the evil genius Imperius Drake, but not before he developed some amazing powers courtesy of Imperius' genetic alterations.

- And of course, Me.

When we are not out scouring the world for evildoers, in cooperation with local, national and international constabularies, we are headquartered in a

16

rambling old mansion near Cincinnati which encompasses not only the Great Bear's opulent digs, but his massive laboratories and shops; his missile silo disguised as an Asian pagoda; and a large Roman temple that serves as a hangar for his three airplanes. We shall wander through that facility several times during our upcoming adventure.

A bit more about the Bearoness. She and Octavius have a hard-to-describe relationship that dates back well prior to Belinda's first marriage and show-biz stardom. They had first met and parted in Churchill, Canada when Belinda Black was still a juvenile and Octavius was a post-doc researcher studying polar bear migration habits. Romance bloomed but then was squashed by Belinda's stage struck mother. Pulling every trick in the *Pushy Mom's Handbook for Promoting Your Star-Struck Offspring (which I suspect she wrote)* she got Belinda a job in the chorus of the Aquabears, a world famous troupe of singing, dancing, swimming, posing Maritime Ursines.

Bearon Byron, himself a polar, took one look at her and fell like the proverbial ton of fish. After a microsecond's hesitation, he bought the review and made Belinda his star attraction. No taking it away from her. She is beautiful and she is a great natural performer who has honed her skills to perfection. She is also one tough sow under that patina of elegance and style. In our previous adventures, she has mixed it up with the bad guys to their significant detriment. A true piece of work, as they say, but not to her face!

Not too long after they had married, Bearon Byron was killed in a skiing accident and left his grieving *(?)* spouse all of his considerable worldly possessions including the Aquabear Review, Bearmoral Castle, a huge pile of funds and a dreadfully dysfunctional family of in-laws. A bit later, Bel and

17

Tavi met again at a charity fete. He was by then a gazillionaire scientific entrepreneur and she was an extremely well-off widow.

The relationship picked up but by now both of these formidable animals had firmly established habits and lifestyles that seemed about to keep them from a final amalgamation. However, love won out and merge they did, but they still haven't settled on where or how they would live together. Octavius is reluctant to be away from his enterprises in Kentucky and his mansion in Cincinnati. Belinda cannot move out of the castle without risking losing it. Hence, for the nonce at least, the shuttle visitations. However, events and individuals are now putting a strain on this arrangement.

Anyway, it is here in Unst in the Shetlands that the ancestors of the late Bearon Byron had established their palatial estate which she had then inherited. She retains the name Bruin in her long list of appellations in order to maintain her bearonial status. In Book Three of this series, you may recall she managed to oust her in-laws and take full control of the estate, chattels and paraphernalia of office. It would seem that settled the case but one never knows.

Actually Bearmoral Castle started out as a theme park. The Bearon's Scottish ancestors only go back three generations. Polar Bears are not indigenous to the Shetlands although the climate suits them just fine. Like Belinda, most of the Bruin family is from Canada although to hear Bel tell it, they acted as if you've fallen off the earth if you travel west of Unst. The first Bearon *(the titles are bought, by the way)* was a canny showman and decided Northern Europe could be a great playground for ursines of all types, especially the polars from the Bearents Sea. He chose Scotland's northernmost land mass for his entrepreneurial endeavor.

The castle began life as a hundred room hotel, spa and open sea swim resort. It did well but the original Bearon's other investments did even better and by the time he died, his arrogant son and daughter decided that the castle should be converted into a sumptuous residence suitable for bears of their breeding, stature, history *(fake)* and wealth *(real.)*

Down came the cutesy neon signs of cuddly polar cubs and up went the heraldic banners along with a mass importation of phony clan symbols, tartans, weapons and other status conscious folderol. Belinda thought the whole thing was a big hoot and just enjoyed the place for what it was. Her in-laws on the other hand, swallowed the fantasy as if it was a school of salmon *(which are excellent up here)* and took on all the obnoxious airs of petty nobility. Most of the locals who know Bel are fond of her and admire her but in general the Bruin "clan" was not much liked. If it wasn't for Belinda's generosity and social conscience, all of the Bearmoral Castle riches would still be locked underneath the moat. They even had a drawbridge that they pulled up at night.

All that has changed again. With the departure *(hasty but complete)* of the "family," Belinda speeded up the timetable to turn the castle back into the resort the first Bearon had in mind. Now, the contractors have mostly packed up and left. **Polar Paradise** will become the playground destination of choice for the northern ursine and other chill-seeking population. Chita, whom you will meet shortly, leveraging her partner position with Belinda, insisted on installing several spas and saunas. That sounded good to me, too.

With the arrival of the twin cubs, Arabella and McTavish, *Polar Paradise* has developed, or I should say re-developed its theme park characteristics with a vengeance and a heavy accent on fun.

19

A carousel was taken down from the parapet where it was stored and re-assembled near the beach. The Bearoness is quite adamant about it being fully restored. The castle's theatre was being taken out of mothballs and the pool has been refurbished to do double duty as a show venue. Some of the original signage was salvaged and new electric and electronic glitz put on order. Much of the Scots décor was being preserved but updated with a "now" look. The moat has been totally cleaned out, refilled with circulating water and the local seals and otters were hired to perform in it several times a day *(weather permitting.)* In fact, the new resort bodes well for the economy and more jobs throughout the Shetlands.

There is now an annex of the now famous Lion and Unicorn pub *(See Book Three – The Case of Scotch)* inside the castle. The idea is not just to sell drinks to the guests. We want to promote the original pub down in Unst village. Statues and pictures of the two worthy hosts, flags, drums, copies of the opening issue of Chita's magazine *Purr* and the matching issue of *Sow* featuring Lion and Unicorn will be on display. And there will be mead, mead and more mead. *(Octavius' contribution.)*

Fiona, the pub's sweet little Dandie Dinmont barmaid has been promoted to manager of the castle's "lounge" and she is busy barking orders at everyone in sight. A tour jitney will run guests back and forth to the original watering spot *(a thrill ride in itself.)* Of course, the two proprietors, Lion and Unicorn, are a major tourist attraction in their own right, complete with crowns and battles.

But now, we come to the star attractions of Polar Paradise. The Twins! Arabella and McTavish Bear, unexpected offspring of Belinda and Octavius. They have set the castle and its occupants on their proverbial ears. Given their parents, it should be no surprise that they are prodigies with capital "Ps." They have everyone who comes in contact with them scratching their fur, hide or pelt in wonderment. Everyone, that is, except for their governess, a no-nonsense Bichon Frisé named Mlle Woof. She it is who maintains sanity and order in this mini-cosmos of high octane energy, wild imagination and super intelligence. The Twins are the jet-powered agents who will take our story on its wild trajectory. Fasten your seat belts.

# The Development of Civilization Volume 5 Part 2

## Hybrids

### *(From "An Introduction to Faunapology" by Octavius Bear PhD.)*

*As we noted in previous commentaries, the evolution of our civilization has undergone many significant variations. Initially, social structures developed within individual species but expanded over time to become subtler, more sophisticated and effective. In this way, over thousands of years, herds, packs, flocks and other intra-species groups developed more intricate systems for establishing and conducting their "business" of living.*

*Other interesting results materialized as inter-species societies began to build. The idea of the greater good began to formulate itself and "society" as a working concept began to emerge. Soon thereafter the even more complex ideas of "preserving (defending) society" developed.*

*Powered by the movement toward societal preservation, organizations evolved. Some were populated by a single species but many consisted of multiple animal varieties, tied to each other by geographic, climatic, and eventually purely social bonds including religion. It was inevitable then, that a certain amount of cross-species breeding would take place in those cases where physical characteristics permitted. Viability of progeny from these matings vary and are, in some instances, quite rare. Even in those cases where the results are viable, the "children" themselves are often sterile.*

*There are many feline variants, especially cross mating of lions, tigers, leopards and smaller cats such as ocelots and servals. Thus far, cheetahs are not known to hybridize. There are several major crossbreeds among equine species including some uncommon horse/zebra combinations. Yaks, cows and buffalos (bisons) have produced hybrid offspring. Some sea borne mammals and sharks have had unique results from inter species mating.*

*Which brings us to the rather remarkable and unexpected results of coupling between The Bearoness Belinda and myself. Our two cubs, Arabella and McTavish are, in the genetic jargon, "poliaks" the result of Polar-Kodiak mating. These two are all the more extraordinary because The Bearoness was believed to be beyond her cub bearing years. Since both Polar and Kodiak bears tend to be hefty and we two are large members of our own species, it was inevitable that our twins would be quite sizeable. We are especially pleased that they are demonstrating amazing intelligence and adaptability. Unfortunately, their energy levels are also extremely high, keeping us and their Bichon Frisé governess on the fine edge of exhaustion.*

# Chapter Two

## *Polar Paradise / Bearmoral Castle*

*Watching over the cubs while they play*
*She corrects and protects them each day.*
*But addressing her, please,*
*Do not say Bichon Freeze.*
*Her name's French and it's Bichon Freezay!*

"What are you talking about? You were the Tomb Raider and I was leading the priests pursuing you. Was there a third player?" This from McTavish.

Arabella replied. "Nobody I know, but there definitely was a snake. A big cobra. I think it was a Uraeus, one of the snakes that protect the tombs of the Pharaohs."

"You and I are running the same level of the game and I didn't see any Uraeus feature or character in the menu. Are you making this up? If you are, I'll swat you!"

"I am not making it up. Anyway, we can't check right now. Mlle Woof will have a major barking fit if we don't get ready for bed.

*(It isn't entirely clear how a small, white, curly haired dog can face down two Polar/Kodiak hybrid bear cubs but she does it and quite effectively. She was recommended to the Bearoness by another member of the Aquabears Revue. Actually, she keeps the entire castle staff and occupants on constant high alert. Canine psychology, I suppose.)*

24

*****

We were having drinks before dinner. "We" being Octavius, Belinda, Frau Schuylkill, Colonel Where, Otto, L. Condor and myself. Octavius was making a serious dent in a keg of mead. The Bearoness was having a bowl of prestige cuvée champagne. Otto was working his way through a vodka and kelp juice. Scotch seemed to be the drink of choice for the others except me. I was once again united with my favorite, fermented coconut milk VSOP. Belinda had discovered an African source and was accommodating me to the fullest. Charming lady!

Octavius has taken to spending more time at the castle since the cubs came on the scene and was devoting much of his time to their mental development. The Bearoness, no intellectual slouch herself, is concentrating on expanding their social skills, leaving deportment and good behavior in the paws of Mlle Woof. The Bichon Frisé is also teaching them languages, not allowing them to take advantage of the UUI Pea Pod Universal Translators. Octavius and Belinda heartily approve. The cubs had scarfed down their dinners earlier and if Mlle Woof was having her way, they would soon be in bed. She would then join us for dinner and if she arrived early enough, a bowl of Sancerre.

Back at the Bear's Lair in Cincinnati, Howard Watt, our brilliant porcupine scientific genius, is holding down the fort and rapidly expanding his work on the Multiverse Project – a major effort devoted to understanding and dealing with the existence of, as we now knew, very real and possibly threatening alternate universes.

I don't know which issue is consuming more of Octavius' attention and concern: the Multiverse or the discovery one year ago by Inspector Bruce

Wallaroo that our long standing nemesis, Imperius Drake is still alive. The duck announced his survival from a mid-air collision with L. Condor over the Ohio River by sending his raucous signature Black Quack ovoid to the Inspector in Australia. No indication of where or how he was. No indication of whether his brainless but brawny assistant, Bigg Baboon, was alive and with him. In short, no indications at all except that stick-it-in-your-eye gesture at Bruce, whom the duck loved to tweak. Time marches on!

So, with the cubs, managing Universal Ursine Industries, working with the Bearoness on Polar Paradise, keeping tabs on Project Multiverse and trying to second guess Imperius Drake, Octavius' plate is overflowing.

Speaking of plates, Dougal, the castle's manager and major domo, announced dinner. Mrs. McRadish, our Shetland sheep cook, and her cloned maids, Dolly, Polly, Holly and Molly once again outdid themselves. Interesting that Frau Schuylkill, a Cordon Bleu chef and culinary empress of Octavius' Cincinnati domain, restrained herself and stayed out of the kitchen. Of course, she and her mate, Colonel Where are also deeply tied up in Multiverse and now the "verdammt duck" is back somewhere and putting the wolves on high alert. Since his poke at Bruce Wallaroo last year, we have heard nothing more from him. We're not betting on him being dormant.

All of this concerns me, of course, as the Great Bear's assistant and field manager but I am also deep into my role as theatrical agent for Bearnice and Bearyl Blanc, polar singer and actress respectively and former flight crew on Belinda's SST, *The Aquabear*. My other clients are Bearnice's singing partner, Leperello, (Lepi) a highly talented Himalayan Snow Leopard and Otto the Magnificent, our illusionist otter, who splits his time working on our crime fighting activities and performing with the Bearoness' aquatic revue, *Some*

26

*Like It Cold*, which will be opening shortly here at Polar Paradise. Bearnice and Lepi are currently on an international tour and Bearyl is playing to overflow audiences as Lady Macbearth. In short, none of us could be accused of idleness. Little did we know!

Octavius turned to Mlle Woof and asked, "What have the little terrors been up to now, Mademoiselle?"

"Oh, Monsieur le Docteur, it is almost frightening how advanced they have become in so short a time. No doubt, the genetic and active influence of La Bearoness and yourself. Tonight, after dinner, they were playing a video game about tombs in Egypt and Arabella insisted that a snake that guarded the tomb of a Pharaoh was approaching her. McTavish would have none of it. As usual, I had to intervene. But ancient Egypt has become their latest passion. I think you must expect to hear from them on the subject, if you haven't already."

Belinda chuckled, "Last week, they wanted to meet the Prince of Whales. They found out you knew him, Tavi, and nothing would do except a promise that they could go out to see him. Will you be hearing from Marlin again now that he's back with the Prince? How did the undersea translator project work out?"

"Quite well," said the Bear. "In fact, after a few changes the Prince wants in order to make it more rugged in undersea depths, the SeaPod will be entering general production. It's a gift from me to him to thank him for his help in solving the oil rig troubles we were having. *(See Book 3, The Case of Scotch)* Actually, Bel, I think he'd enjoy meeting the cubs. We still have to negotiate whether we can get Marlin, who is about the most brilliant dolphin I have ever met, permanently transferred to us. He'd be a natural here in the

Polar Paradise. And he's done some fine work with Howard on Project Multiverse."

"Pardon, Monsieur le Docteur, but I have heard you mention this Multiverse Project a number of times. What is it?"

"Mademoiselle, a long answer would take days to unfold and explain. Let's just say that we have uncovered significant evidence that our world and universe are not the only ones in the cosmos. We have encountered individuals living in other worlds. Some of them seem relatively benign and are not aware of us here on Earth. But, recently we uncovered some facts that make us believe that there are one or more worlds that are conscious of us, and have even sent individuals to take up residence here. We are not convinced of their good intentions. All this is highly confidential. I mean that most emphatically. We have confined this knowledge thus far to an extremely small group but it will no doubt spread."

"Mon Dieu," barked the Bichon, "are the cubs in danger?"

"Your concern for the cubs is admirable, Mademoiselle," said Belinda. "I appreciate it no end. The fact is, we don't know. It seems only a small number of individuals have visited Earth. Thus far, they have been advanced animals like ourselves. We are concerned that *Homo Sapiens* may also be involved although they would have great difficulty remaining unobserved here."

"The same *Homo Sapiens* that died out here hundreds of thousands of years ago?"

This time L. Condor joined the discussion. "We don't have enough evidence to be certain but the ones we have seen come close. The Colonel has had the most experience with them along with Dr. Bear's half brother Agrippa. What do you think, Colonel?"

"It's tough to tell. I can't help thinking that like us, they have probably evolved over that period but that's what Project Multiverse is all about. Trying to answer questions like the ones you are asking and being prepared for any eventuality. You have not met Doctor Howard Watt, our principal scientist on the project. He is extremely competent and has been filling in the picture quite effectively."

"Meanwhile, Mademoiselle," said Octavius, "we have lives to live; cubs to raise; hotels and major industries to manage; crimes and criminals to handle; and much to my chagrin, probably demon ducks to contend with."

The Bichon Frisé thought better of asking about demon ducks but she was becoming increasingly convinced that she had taken on an assignment that was not going to be at all routine. Little did *she* know what awaited her! Neither did we!

Imperius Drake

# Chapter Three

## *A Nondescript Island in the Red Sea*

*Say hello to Imperius Drake!*
*To ignore him would be a mistake.*
*He spends all of his time*
*Plotting new forms of crime.*
*Yes, Imperius Drake is a flake.*

"Sire, we've been here over a year. When are we going to leave this place? I don't like it here."

"Baboon, we will leave when we have completed our preparations for the Great Pharaonic Restoration. Once more the name of Imperius Drake, Lord of the Universes, will be proclaimed wherever beings draw breath."

"When was the last time, Sire?"

"When was the last time…what?"

"When your name was proclaimed wherever beings draw breath?"

"A figure of speech, Baboon.'

"Imperius" is the nom-de-crime of Doctor Yu-Aul-Kum, a Mandarin Duck and former scientist at the Pan Asia Institute for Avian Advancement. A brilliant chemist, geneticist, physicist, biologist, and developmental psychiatrist, he devoted his early life to the genetic enhancement of bird brains, creating a serum that would create a race of "Super Anitidae" – the über ducks.

He made his experiments known in a series of papers delivered before the International Genetics Experts Society. He was roasted. The society chairman, *Il Professore* Roberto Rabbito, a self-important Italian white rabbit with Noble prizes on his brain, singled him out for scathing derision.

Mocked by his fellow scientists worldwide, shunned by medical and professional journals, and threatened by government functionaries, Yu-Aul-Kum fled to the highlands of Nepal with his adoring mate and fellow scientist, Lee-Li-Li. There, after long contemplation under the direction of the Dalai Duck, he began to work again. In desperation, he began performing experiments on himself.

The experiments showed promise. Every week, he re-tested his IQ, synapses and reflexes. He was getting smarter. He was quicker. His eyesight was enhanced. He could fly higher, longer and perform breathtaking aerobatics. In a power dive, he once chased a falcon to the ground, caught him and then…killed him.

Yes, killed him. A mild-mannered duck wiped out a fearsome bird of prey. He felt a surge of power building up in his body and psyche. He was becoming the Über-Duck Archetype.

He was also becoming a menace. Sometimes after an especially risky trial, he could feel his body change along with his mind. His beautifully hued feathers turned black. His crest flattened. His eyes took on a piercing stare. His wings shook and trembled. His "quack" was sharp and rasping. He ate ravenously.

And…he frightened Lee-Li-Li. This was no longer the devoted mate she had loved. This wasn't the high-minded scientist she had so admired. No longer did she hear him discourse on the importance of bettering life for avians. He was turning into a loon.

Over and over, she tried to get him to abandon, or at least redirect his work. The Duck would have none of it. "So close, so close! I'll show those unbelieving nitwits who has a big head. They'll come begging me to allow them to assist in my great work, and I will laugh at them as they laughed at me. I am almost there, Lee, almost there. Just a few more tweaks to the formula, and I'll be ready. We'll have to find some stray dodos to experiment with. If it works on them, it'll work on anyone."

Just when he believed he was finally going to achieve total success, Lee-Li-Li, fearful for his life and sanity, burned his lab notes and swallowed their entire supply of the serum, sacrificing herself to prevent his self-destruction. The serum worked, expanding her intelligence by a factor of 5000, but the overdose burned out her brain and she died in his wings while solving once and for all, Schrödinger's dilemma of quantum indeterminacy.

Maddened by his loss and swearing vengeance against all his foes, real and imagined, Yu-Aul-Kum has since reconstructed his notes and the serum and with each dose transforms himself into the scourge of modern civilization – Imperius Drake. The temporary reconstitution is astounding – not only does his intelligence rise well beyond the scale of any known animal including dolphins, but his vindictiveness and hatred are also without equal. The transformation is made complete by a stark change in his physical appearance, morphing from the multi-hued beauty of the Mandarin species to a somber, black, and ominous winged predator whose maniacal "quack" stirs panic in the hearts and souls of all who hear it.

But before he could reach this pinnacle of achievement, he needed a new start. Armed with super endurance and GPS, and reverting to his natural Mandarin guise, Yu-Aul-Kum flew to the North American continent to begin his campaign of global revenge. Here he knew he could find the facilities, money, and support he required. But he must be careful. Using yet another alias, he applied and was accepted at the Genetics Science unit of Octavius Bear's Universal Ursine Industries. There he amazed his colleagues and superiors with his knowledge, technique, and almost inexhaustible energy. They gave him more and more responsible projects, and he was soon able to gain all the access he needed to equipment and processes to support his dreams of conquest.

Then, for the first time, he encountered Octavius Bear. The Bear was on a routine personal audit of the Genetics Science facilities at UUI. Going through the work-in- progress reports, he discovered a massive development project for which no executive authorization existed. Octavius literally hit the ceiling. It was the Duck! Caught out in his nefarious deeds and transmuting into his evil counter-self, Imperius Drake attacked Octavius with a lab knife. Octavius had been attacked before, certainly, but never by a...duck (?) The two of them engaged in raucous thrust and parry. Imperius landed several major wounds on the Bear's legs and body. Octavius flailed wildly, and truth be told, it was he who wreaked the most extensive damage on the UUI labs. Fortunately, the Great Ursine just bearly survived the Duck's onslaught and threw the maddened canard through a plate glass window four stories up. Thus began the ceaseless battle between Imperius and Octavius. Believed to be

34

killed several times, the Duck has thus far returned even stronger in his desire for revenge. Only his desire for world conquest outstrips his personal vendetta with the Great Bear. Nirvana would be achieved by conquering both the cosmos and the despicable ursine in one blow. Such is the plan he is now hatching.

"At last we have reached the point in our research and development where we can summon the Great Pharaoh Tsk VI, the ancient Egyptian king hippopotamus, from the Underworld Universe where he currently dwells."

"Isn't he dead, Sire?"

"Only in a manner of speaking, Baboon. While he was being mummified, he passed on to another world where he still reigns as leader of the Languishing Leonine Legions and the Crocodiles of the Pharaoh's Phalanx. He and they have been confined to that Underworld for centuries, without any hope of returning to his former realm. We shall now make that possible."

"Why?"

"Conquest, Baboon, conquest! We shall reproduce his immortal armies and use them to overwhelm not just this paltry globe but the entire cosmos."

"Is he going to let you do that, Sire?"

"It will be one of the major conditions for his being brought back. Of course, he will believe that once re-established here on Earth, it will be a simple matter to overwhelm and dispose of me. He will be seriously mistaken. In fact, once I have taken over his supporters and armies and multiplied them through genetic manipulation, it is he who will become redundant. This time I will make sure that he truly perishes."

"How?"

"By means too complex for you to understand, Baboon."

Bigg, once again, felt anger at the duck for his nasty condescension. *(I'm not sure Bigg knew what condescension was or how to spell it but he was annoyed. Readers of Book Two – The Case of the Spotted Band may remember Bigg fantasizing about being the Emperor instead of Imperius. Lately, that fantasy was returning more strongly and with greater frequency.)*

"Maybe I would understand, Duck" he said.

Imperius was momentarily taken aback. To be called "Duck" by the Baboon was not only unusual but possibly even menacing. Clearly, it was time for him to create a new Black Quack Gang. Restricted to himself, Chita and Bigg Baboon, the original gang had prospered and had been propelled to new heights of dastardly fame and fortune.

But then things began to unravel. Chita had been a mistake from the start. She had joined Imperius under duress and was willing to stay on only as long as she was amply compensated and free to act on her own. Her streak of independence could not be subjugated by chemistry. Unfortunately, his attempts to kill her several times had not been successful. Clearly, the cat had multiple lives. And she hated the Duck.

He attempted to replace her with a hapless performing otter. Working his genetic skills, he altered the nature of the lutrine and created Otto the Magnificent, gifted with the abilities to escape from constraints, move at lightning speed and perform telekinetic feats at will.

But his efforts to bring Otto under his total influence did not turn out well, either. No doubt due to inherent shortcomings in the otter's basic nature and temperament. Imperius' work on the otter's DNA was flawless. It was, of course, the subject who was at fault.

*(Such was Imperius' colossal ego that it would never occur to him that he was the stumbling block in bringing his plots to successful conclusions. His formidable intelligence, amplified by the serum he had been taking, lo, these many years, was offset by his total failure to accept any personal responsibility for the debacles he had unleashed. In dealing with the Dastardly Duck, Octavius and his team counted on Imperius' genius for pulling defeat from the jaws of victory. So far, it had worked. Who knows?)*

Now Bigg was showing strange new signs of discontent and possible rebellion. Imperius must search carefully for new associates.  The Great Pharaonic Restoration was too important to be upended by slipshod or mutinous behavior. He must have total, unwavering, enthusiastic, highly competent, unquestioning obedience and support. Anything less was unthinkable.

A few compliments and rewards tossed at Bigg might restore him to his mindless acquiescence but that would only suffice for the moment. New blood would be necessary but it must be carefully chosen and indoctrinated. He would need aides who were expert in Egyptology, and ruthless, but still needy enough to be willing to subject themselves to his will.  He would give them apparent freedom of action and rewards but always ensure they knew and appreciated wherein the power rested. The search must begin.

*****

Meanwhile, in Sydney, Inspector Bruce Wallaroo was packing his travel gear and heading for the airport and the long trek to the Shetlands. Nothing motivated the marsupial as much as his hatred for "that damn duck"

37

and a desire to see him finished off for good. He had just signed off on a call to Octavius. They agreed that Imperius was once again a high priority item, and that Bruce would be a most welcome addition to the Polar Paradise contingent. Besides, he had never met the cubs. We had better brace ourselves. Bruce and the cubs! Hurricane Category Five or above. The Shetlands may not be ready for the blast. But, the whirlwinds would have to contend with the dampening influences of Frau Schuylkill and now also, Mlle Woof. I'd call it a potential draw but entertaining nonetheless.

# Chapter Four

## *Polar Paradise*

*A discovery made by the twins*
*Raises goose-bumps on most of our skins.*
*A royal cobra appears,*
*Giving vent to her fears.*
*And so our adventure begins.*

Thumps and Bumps! Two brown and white, fur covered projectiles bounced out of the family wing elevator and streaked toward the kitchen. Breakfast called, nay shouted, and they shouted back. Arabella and McTavish, sixteen months old and hybrids both, were virtually identical twins. Only a small patch of brown on McTavish's left ear distinguished him from his sister. It was a source of constant discussion as to whether they looked more Polar or Kodiak. Their bodies were covered in distinctive polar white as were their legs except for brown socks that appeared on all four of their feet. Their faces were primarily dark brown with white circles surrounding their eyes. Their ears were white with the aforementioned brown spot on McTavish's port side. It was clear they were going to be sizeable adults like their parents. Their facial structure favored Octavius with a narrower and more elongated nose than was typical of polars. They moved rapidly and jumped almost constantly. In short, they were cubs. Highly intelligent cubs as they were about to demonstrate.

Mlle Woof, Mrs. McRadish and the maids surrounded them and herded them toward large bowls of fish.

"Where's Poppa Bear, Mlle Woof," shouted McTavish. "We need to tell him about the snake. I think he wants to communicate with us. He just appeared on Bella's screen. He wasn't supposed to be there. He wants something and we think Poppa and Momma just have to meet him."

"Your parents are busy, mes petites. They don't have time for playing your video games."

"But they have to. They just have to!" squealed Arabella.

"What do we have to?" Belinda had just entered the room.

"You and Poppa have to talk to the snake." A bear cub chorus.

"Who is this snake?"

"We don't know but he seems to be terribly important. He's guarding the Pharaoh's tomb."

"But it's all make believe, isn't it?"

"No, it's not! It's not! Please Momma!

"All right! All right! Mademoiselle, will you please find Octavius. Thank you. But I warn you two. If this some of your silliness, there will be consequences.

"We're not being silly. Really we're not. We talked with him this morning and he needs to consult with the great seeker of justice, Dr. Octavius Bear. That's exactly what he said. Is Poppa really a great seeker of justice? What's justice?"

"It means ensuring that the right things are done and that animals who hurt others or try to do terrible things are kept from doing them. If they do bad things, then they should be found out and punished."

"When we do something you think is wrong, you punish us. I was stealing treasure from the tomb in the game and I almost got caught. I guess I would have been punished for that if Tavi could have caught me. Is that justice?"

"Yes, but Poppa is usually involved in things that are much more serious and harmful. Someone once tried to kill Momma and Poppa stopped him."

"Oh, Momma, really?? Were you hurt? Did Poppa punish him? Is he still alive? Will he try to kill us?"

Belinda immediately regretted the way the conversation had turned. "You don't have to worry. Momma and Poppa are here to protect you."

"But who protects you and Poppa?"

"We're quite good at protecting ourselves. And we have a lot of help from Mlle Woof, Frau Schuylkill and Colonel Where and Uncle Maury and Howard and L. Condor. Otto is extremely good at protecting, too. And there's somebody you're going to meet tomorrow. Inspector Bruce Wallaroo. He's from Australia. Do you know where Australia is?"

"Mademoiselle Woof taught us about the different continents. Australia is awfully far away. Is he coming to see us?"

"Oh, yes! He's been wanting to meet you ever since you were born. He's a lot of fun. You'll love him."

"We've never seen a wallaroo."

"You're in for a treat."

Belinda tried to steer clear of Imperius Drake and Bigg. But the fact that the duck was still alive and no doubt, just as threatening or even worse did not give her much consolation. No, the twins would have to learn about him but not right now. They'll probably overhear the discussions when Bruce arrived.

The Bichon had found Octavius and he trundled into the room, obviously not in the best of moods. Some issue at Universal Ursine Industries had him upset.

"All right, you two! What's this foolishness about the snake in your video game? Yesterday, it was the Prince of Whales I was supposed to introduce you to. Now it's some dead Egyptian King's guardian I have to talk to. You certainly seem to like royalty."

"It's not foolishness, Poppa. I think the snake's name is Uraeus. He guards the tomb of King Tsk VI. He showed up on Arabella's game monitor last night and we were talking to him again this morning. He wants to speak to you about seeking justice. We don't know what it's about but he insists it's you he wants to talk to. Momma has already told us we'll be in a lot of trouble if this is some kind of joke but it's not, Poppa. It's not!"

"All right, let's get this over with. C'mon, Bel. You're going to have to deal with these two if this doesn't turn out to be what I think it is. Some joker who hacked into Bella's game console and now has them bouncing off the walls."

Arabella clapped her paws together and ran off to get the family wing elevator. Octavius, Belinda, Mlle Woof and I *(remember me, Maury?)* followed after McTavish as he raced back and forth between the elevator and

42

us, trying to move the parade along. Arabella had captured the lift so we had to wait for the car's return.

McTavish said, "The snake talks funny, Poppa. He hisses a lot. He's big and he has shiny red eyes. He's a cobra, I think, and he has a gold hood. Oh, here's the lift. Hurry, everybody! We don't want to keep him waiting."

The cubs had obviously bought into this whole thing very seriously. If it was a hacker's prank, they were in for a big disappointment.

Once in their rooms, Octavius walked over to the game unit and stared at the screen. If this was a hack, it was damn sophisticated.

Arabella spoke. "Hello, Uraeus!"

Sssss! Greetings, youthful bear. Where is your sibling?

"Here I am! Here I am! Our Momma and Poppa are with us and so are Uncle Maury and Mlle Woof."

"I welcome you all. Please come around so I may look at you. Aahh! A beautiful bear of the polar species. The Pharaoh kept one but he was not of the advanced sort such as you all are. Is that true? Little white dog! Are you a pet?"

Wrong thing to say to Mlle Woof. A growl rumbled in her throat. "No, snake. I am the governess of the ursine twins. I am well educated and well experienced in many arts, including self defense and protection. Do not let my small and curly haired appearance mislead you. Indeed, I might ask the same of you. Who and what are you?"

"A thousand pardons. In the remote regions of the desert, one does not have much opportunity to practice the social niceties. I am the guardian of the

43

realm of King Tsk VI, powerful Pharaoh and greatly feared lord. It is here where his mummified mortal shell resides under my protection. It is through that shell and his tomb that I am capable of seeing and hearing beings and events in other worlds. I also have full access to the Underworld where at the moment, the Pharaoh's spirit continues in his deep sleep, and where his Languishing Leonine Legions and his Pharaoh's Phalanx patiently await his awakening and call to action. Thousands of your years have passed since he has been aroused. But now I see several other beings here, one of whom I hope is the Powerful Seeker of Justice."

Since he clearly didn't mean me, a lowly meerkat, I naturally deferred to Octavius.

The Great Bear stared back at the cobra and said, "I am Octavius Bear. I have been called many things in my lifetime but Powerful Seeker of Justice is not one of them."

*(As those of you who have read the previous Casebooks of Octavius Bear will know all too well, modesty is not one of his outstanding virtues and sure enough, once again, he came through like the champ he is.)*

"However, I suppose the epithet fits. I am physically and mentally far advanced, extremely wealthy and renowned throughout the world. As for seeking justice, it has been my lifelong vocation. I am also no one's fool and at the moment, I view you, your claims and your appearance with great skepticism. I will admit that a great deal of sophisticated design went into creating an avatar such as yourself but while you have clearly captivated our cubs, you have not convinced me. Just what do you want and why me?"

Arabella and McTavish were taken aback by their father's reaction to their wonderful discovery but before they could protest, Belinda took them to

44

a corner of the room and said, "Your father knows what he's doing. He's been dealing with strange and dangerous animals all his life. I'm sure you're dazzled by this creature but your father and I are not. A least not yet. I don't think Uncle Maury and Mlle Woof are convinced, either. Don't worry, we'll give Uraeus the benefit of the doubt for the moment while we find out what he wants but if he's a danger to you or just a harmless fake, he will have wished he hadn't made an appearance."

"But, Momma…"

"Hush, go over and sit quietly with Mlle Woof…NOW!"

The cubs had learned how to roll their eyes at an early age and applied that skill as they shuffled over to their waiting governess. Mlle Woof said nothing but put her paw to her mouth, signaling silence and nodding toward Octavius.

I often disappear off the landscape when standing next Octavius so I decided to intervene.

"My name is Maury Meerkat and I am a highly trusted aide to Doctor Bear, Bearoness Belinda and the two cubs. You and I share African roots and have the desert as part of our bloodlines. Do you have a title? As I understand it, Uraeus is symbolic of the Pharaoh's authority and your role is protection. Can you spit fire from your red eyes? Are you a god or goddess? Are you Wadjet?"

Octavius stared at me as if I had lost my mind but then it occurred to him that maybe there was method in my madness. My questions were designed to throw the snake off in its control of the situation. It worked.

45

"So, little meerkat, you know something of us guardians. Well and good! Let us convince your ursine associate that I am not a fraud or a danger to his house. I come from a noble and powerful dynasty and I do not seek assistance lightly. It is his past history that has persuaded me to seek you all out. To answer your questions, I am a demi-goddess. No, I am not Wadjet. She is my aunt. Like her, I am called the eye of Ra. You may call me Raamjet. Yes, I am female. Yes, I can spit fire from my eyes and deadly venom from my mouth. My fangs are also venomous and my coils can squeeze out life."

At this point, the cubs and Mlle Woof were goggle eyed. Belinda had a quizzical look on her face and I was pretty impressed. Not so, The Great Bear.

Octavius had put up long enough with being upstaged. Rising to his full nine-foot height, he nudged me aside and with a stentorian roar, announced. "We can reserve our exploration of the Egyptian pantheon and celestial attributes until we get a few basics straightened out. Now, at the moment, the only claim you have made that is of interest to me is your knowledge of my past history. Explain yourself and quickly."

The snake reared back. If the video screen didn't separate us, I would have fully expected a venomous spit. Would the screen filter out the fiery eyes? I didn't want to find out. A pause. A long hiss.

"I shall return at a time of my own choosing. Perhaps then you will be more respectful and less cynical. Meanwhile, I will leave you with two words: *Imperius Drake!*"

# Chapter Five

## *The Bear's Lair-Cincinnati and Polar Paradise*

*On separate and quite different fronts,*

*We are waging our Multiverse hunts.*

*But Imperius Drake*

*And a guardian snake*

*Have us chasing more worlds all at once.*

Howard Watt, porcupine techie genius, is once again holding down the fort at The Bear's Lair – Octavius' huge mansion, laboratory, hangar and launch-pad complex not far from the Ohio River. Across the river is the Northern Kentucky based headquarters of Universal Ursine Industries, the wholly-owned business base of Octavius' mega billion fortune. Out of UUI's labs, offices, conference rooms and production facilities have come devices, technologies and scientific wonders that have been acknowledged worldwide as leaders in their class. Governments, institutions, businesses, private individuals all owe major elements of their progress and advancements to UUI. Readers of Book One – *The Open and Shut Case* – will be familiar with the genetics activities at the lab and the clashes that involved Imperius Drake and the Black Quack gang. *(The same Imperius Drake whose name was dropped by Raamjet before her angry departure from Arabella's play console in the previous chapter.)*

Another technical wonder that became a source of extreme and highly dangerous conflict was a device – The Portable Endoatmospheric Particle

Beam Projector. That name is just too long to keep repeating and PEPBP is unpronounceable. So, we call it "the gun" and let the particles fall where they may. Somewhat like a laser but far more powerful, accurate, portable, flexible and selective, a development copy was stolen from the UUI Labs by Imperius Drake. He then used the gun to destroy a priceless sapphire at a Chicago art exhibit, and intended to use it as a weapon of mass destruction on one thousand genetics specialists attending a convention in Las Vegas. Narrowly foiled in the attempt by Octavius and his team, we thought he had been killed in the melee. No such luck. He escaped death yet again at the end of Book Two *(or so we are told by Inspector Bruce Wallaroo, soon to be introduced.)*

But back to Howard Watt, who was heavily involved with the enhancement and protection of the UUI version of "the gun." At the moment, Howard is spearheading a different effort in spite of Octavius' constant micromanagement – The Multiverse Project. You may remember the brief description The Great Bear gave to Mlle Woof at the end of Chapter Two. Stick around. Lots more Multiverse to come!

Howard has devoted a massive amount of time, effort and expertise compiling evidence in support of the existence and nature of multiple worlds and universes beyond our own. Until recently, he was assisted by Marlin, a brilliant dolphin from the court of the Prince of Whales. Marlin has now returned to the Prince armed with the SeaPod, an underwater universal translator developed by UUI. It's a gift for the Prince to thank him for previous favors. Octavius and Howard both hope they can soon call back and permanently attach Marlin to The Great Bear's staff.

While by no means complete, the results of the Multiverse Project have done much to confirm our beliefs that our world, Earth, is not alone. We have found major evidence of animals, both advanced and primitive, in other physical and virtual venues. Furthermore, there is significant support for the theory that our long lost species, *Homo Sapiens,* exists and thrives in some of these places.

One of the dilemmas facing the team is the conflicting need to gather as much data as possible while restricting the project to the smallest number of participants. We try to avoid certain organizations like the quasi military group simply called The Business. Under the direction of an aggressive, super-radical horse named General Turmoil, The Business ostensibly doesn't exist. Its activities include an assortment of spying, clandestine exercises, influencing and coercing governments, corporations, universities, research facilities, and important individuals. Octavius falls into several of those categories and there is little love lost between him and the General. At one point, Colonel Wyatt Where was an unwilling participant in a project not dissimilar to Multiverse, run by The Business and aimed at using alternate worlds as platforms for conquest. Fortunately, it failed but left the Colonel with some rather interesting skills in alternate universe travel. You'll meet Wyatt again shortly.

Howard's encrypted phone rang. No doubt it was Octavius who took no cognizance of time differences *(five hours)* days or dates. Octavius also roared when using a speakerphone, making confidentiality on his end a bit unlikely.

"Howard? *(Who else?)* This is Octavius *(Again, who else?)* How are things going? *(Well, I...)* Listen, I have a top-priority task for you. *(As usual!)* I want you to uncover everything there is to know about the nature and existence of the ancient Egyptian Underworld, most specifically as it applies to the Pharaoh, King Tsk VI. We have had a strange incident here with a snake called Raamjet, supposedly a Uraeus guarding the king's tomb, which I gather is the entrance to his realm in the Underworld. I'm still not convinced that this isn't some sort of hacker's trick. However, she *(yes, she's female)* rattled my cage seriously when she signed off in a huff while dropping the name of Imperius Drake. I'm not sure you've heard he's alive. Bruce Wallaroo got a Black Quack egg last year and now is on his way here to consult with us about him. After the snake calms down, I expect her to return. She's using the cubs' video game to communicate. I gather she wants my help but I'm not sure why. If it involves that crazy duck, this could be a major event. Call me back as soon as you get anything." (Click!)

*****

At the edge of the parking lot at Polar Paradise, an aerial ballet was in its last stages of a *cabriole*. A helicopter in the Aquabears livery was bobbing over a fixed point and swaying from vertical to horizontal and back. The *danseur noble* at the controls was none other than the irrepressible and perpetually mobile Inspector Bruce Wallaroo. The madcap marsupial is also in possession of one of the finest anti-crime brains on the planet. He has joined Octavius and members of his team on a number of adventures and will be all too familiar to readers of the previous Casebooks. Deciding that he had sufficiently announced his presence to a startled ground crew, palace staff and other onlookers, he summarily dropped the craft to the tarmac, cut the engines

50

and barely missing the still moving rotor, bounced out of the door and hopped across the apron. Spotting me, he yowled, "Maury, my old mate. Great to see ya!"

*(As narrator-in-chief of this opus, I must now insert myself briefly into this role to explain a small service I will be supplying to you. With his all but incomprehensible Strine lingo raining on one's ears in super high speed bursts, the Inspector is often unintelligible or worse. Henceforth, I will be translating, transliterating and otherwise making sensible to the non-Australian English reader, Bruce's conversation, outbursts and monologues. I will insert the occasional Ozzie phrase just to keep you aware of his linguistic leanings.)*

Extricating myself from his muscular grasp, *(He's twice my size and four times my weight.)* I said, "Hey Bruce, you're a welcome sight. I thought you'd be south of the equator for a good long while. Nothing like a Black Quack to get you on the move."

"Too right, Maury. Here we were thinking we'd heard the last of the Drongo Duck and he's back front and center. Yer right! Nothing like that perishing black egg to stir the emotions. Where is everybody? Who is everybody?"

"Second question first. Besides the castle staff, the current cast at Polar Paradise includes Octavius, Belinda, Frau Ilse, Colonel Where, Otto, Condo and me. And of course, the twins, Arabella and McTavish and their Bichon Frisé governess, Mlle Woof. The kids are a real hoot. Ever since they heard you were coming, we've been bombarded with 'Is he here yet? Is he here yet?' I'm not sure which of you has the biggest bounce."

"Now your first question. Belinda is with the cubs. Last I heard, Octavius was on the phone with Howard back at The Lair. Not sure where the Frau, Colonel or Condo are. Otto is probably working out in the new pool. Wait till you see the changes the Bearoness and Octavius have wrought upon this place. It's gone from feudal to fun."

"Well, I hear it sure wasn't fun with the Bearon's relatives hanging on. Are they all gone?"

"Oh yeah! The ones who weren't arrested for sabotaging the oil rigs were summarily tossed out on their polar tails by the Bearoness. That was quite an event. Listening to Lady Albearta sputtering and roaring as she was shown the door with all her chattels was worth the price of admission. Off she went with Alistair's stuffed body in tow. I haven't the slightest idea where they are now. Probably back near the Bering Sea. That's where they came from. Look, here comes Octavius."

The Great Bear came out over the drawbridge with his huge paws extended. "Bruce, wonderful to see you. I thought you were tied up in Interpol related work."

"I was and I am, but when that blasted egg appeared quacking up a storm, I put in for leave. Unfortunately, it took a while! The damned duck must still be alive and I want him certifiably dead. I also want to see the end of that stupid baboon, if he's still around. So, where else should I go to make that happen but to return to my old mates? Is Chita here?"

52

"Not yet, but we expect her." I said. *(Frown from Octavius.)*

"Truth be told, I missed you folks and I wanted to see what this fabulous new resort looked like. Besides, there are a couple of youngsters I need to meet."

"And they want to meet you. They're not quite sure wallaroos are real, especially wallaroos who are Police Inspectors."

"Chief Inspector, if you please!"

"Wonderful," shouted Octavius and slapped him on the back, knocking the marsupial off his long flat feet. "Sorry, Chief Inspector, I sometimes don't know my own strength."

I helped the dazed 'roo back up and brushed him off. Sure enough, the badge he was wearing proclaimed, "Detective Chief Inspector."

"That's great, Bruce, and long overdue. Here comes Dougal. He and the other staff will get your kit up to your room and we can sit and chat. It may be too early for a drink, but I'm not sure what time zone you're in at the moment."

"Maury, there is no time zone required for a beer and that flight made me thirsty. When am I going to have you as a chopper passenger again? *(An event not to be imagined or desired. Readers of prior Casebooks will remember my near death experiences flying with Bruce in helicopters. He and they are kindred spirits: soaring, looping, bouncing, hovering, racing off in every available dimension. That's also Bruce by himself. The whirlybird is just*

53

*an extension of his exuberance and enough to keep my nerves and stomach on high alert.)*

I grinned weakly and mumbled something about seeing what the future will bring. We made our way into the palace forecourt, through the drawbridge over the moat, and into the newly decorated and refurbished Polar Paradise lobby.

Bruce let out a loud whistle. "I never saw the castle in its old form but this is a ridgy-didge Taj Mahal."

His whistle attracted the attention of the Dandie Dinmont Terrier who managed the Castle lounge, an annex of the Lion and Unicorn pub in Unst. "Aye sirs, and can I be of service? Hello agin, Doctor Bear. I o'course ken what you and Mister Meerkat are drinkin' but I dinna think I've met this gentlebeast."

"This is Chief Inspector Bruce Wallaroo from Australia, Fiona. He'll be our guest for quite a while. What'll it be, Bruce?"

"Anything that looks and tastes like beer, the stronger, the better!"

"Aye, sir! We have a large assortment of beers. Why don't we let you work your way though the menu until you find something you really like."

"A dog after my own heart, Fiona."

As we settled into a corner spot in the lounge that Octavius had already claimed as his own, Bruce said, "When am I going to meet your young bairns? I never would have guessed you two could or would have cubs."

54

"Neither did we, but Belinda brought them on and they are a fine pair. Bright as stars and absolutely full of motion and mischief. You'll see them shortly, but tell me about the Black Quack. I thought we'd never see or hear one of them again."

"Neither did I, Ocko. What a shock! It drove Sydney headquarters right into the harbour, which is where the damned thing is right now. Killin' the fish, I suppose. Can't be helped."

"Was there any message tied to it. Imperius is not one to restrain his ego."

"Not a bloody word. Just the egg in the box. It started quackin' the minute they opened it in the demolition area. Not taking any chances! But instead of a bomb or a dud, they got the screamer. No regs to cover that one. It was addressed to me. I told them to sink it in the harbour immediately."

"Any return address?"

"Nothing, but we tracked it back to the courier service that delivered it and checked out their logs. We got the country of origin. Ready for this?"

"What?"

**"Egypt!"**

# Chapter Six

## *That same nondescript Red Sea island*

*The Mad Duck will be gone for a while*
*As he leaves the Red Sea for the Nile.*
*He'll be spending his time*
*Seeking partners in crime*
*To assist in his venture so vile.*

"I must go to the mainland, Baboon. I shall probably be gone for several days. You meanwhile, must maintain the security of this sanctum and keep unwelcome noses from prying into our sacred work."

"What is our sacred work, sire?"

"The Great Pharaonic Restoration, of course"

"Oh, that!"

"Yes, that. Keep yourself busy. Practice shooting the ray gun. You enjoy that. Since I have restored it, I have not had time to totally test it. I am certain that I have improved it far beyond the pitiable capabilities of the Bear's primitive model. Just make sure you keep your activities secret and report your results to me when I return. I must fly down to the dock and take the launch over to the village."

"OK, but first I'm going to have my lunch here."

The Duck sighed and headed for the wharf.

Beyond the core of the Black Quack Gang, Imperius Drake alters the number and composition of his associates to fit whatever dirty deed he is planning at the particular moment. And he always has an ample supply of willing contractors and mercenaries on every continent ready and waiting to do his bidding.

Here in Egypt, he would be interviewing potential henchbeings to assist him in his assault on the tomb of King Tsk VI. It is critical that he overpower the Uraeus that guards the tomb and capture the King's Book of the Dead. The Book describes the path to the Underworld taken by the Pharaoh, along with the incantations necessary to assuage his keepers, such as Anubis, the Jackal God of Mummification. Armed with the Book, he will then arouse the hippopotamus from his long sleep and present him with his plans of world conquest. No doubt, his clever persuasiveness will convince the King to arouse his Languishing Leonine Legions and Pharaonic Phalanx to once more go forth and dominate the known world.

There is the crux of the Duck's nefarious plan. The Known World! He must persuade Tsk that in order to re-establish his power over a far more extensive realm, he must first allow Imperius to use his genetic arts and sciences to expand and enhance his armies; adjust them to present day environments and organize them for global, nay, cosmic conquest. He must get himself appointed as the King's Vizier, the most trusted member of the court and once established, slowly and subtly displace the Pharaoh as the true leader of the newly restored Egyptian Dynasty. No doubt, there will be some individuals, especially high ranking officers, who will not trust the Duck and may challenge his authority and influence. They will be converted or eliminated. Imperius was supremely confident of his ability to overcome and to lead. *(Where had we heard that before?)*

But all this is in the future. For the moment, he must re-establish contact with his long-time associate in transgressions, Effendi, who has at his claws, an electronic database of the crème-de-la-crème of criminality. The vulture, for such he is, had in the past supplied Imperius with temporary help for a wide range of anti social activities. They were usually effective, if a bit costly. But this initiative calls for much more selectivity and scrutiny. That is why, for the first time, they would be meeting, beak to beak, in a small bistro in Armant, near but not too near Luxor.

Flying over the desert separating the Red Sea and the Nile, he rehearsed in his mind the characteristics required for the assignment. First and foremost, the aspirant needed a deep, demonstrated knowledge of Egyptology, especially the Tsk dynasty. The Tsk pharaohs were all hippos with the extraordinary aggressiveness inherent in the breed. Tsk VI, if the lore was to be believed, was the archetype. His foes all shared a common fate: complete and horrific destruction. Lost in a sinking barge, his death marked the end of the era for the strangely named "river horses." Subsequent royalty sprang from more peaceful and benign strains until Egypt was ultimately conquered by Roman forces. Never again had there arisen a leader of such ferocity and malice. Tsk VI was truly the unique candidate to underpin the Duck's ambitions for cosmic conquest.

A second and even more demanding item on the Duck's list of "hench being traits" was a proven history of successful discoveries, thefts and smuggling of royal artifacts. No amateurs need apply. It was crucial that Imperius gain control of the Pharaoh's Book of the Dead – the all important access mechanism to the King's spiritual resting place in the Underworld. He believed the book still existed among the funerary objects in King Tsk's tomb but under the unwavering eye of a Uraeus, a magnificent and maleficent cobra charged with protecting the royal mummy and all of his worldly possessions. The snake would fall victim to the enhanced particle beam weapon. That would remain the Baboon's task, assuming he could still be trusted.

Crossing the Nile to the west bank, he circled Armant until he caught sight of the most disreputable looking tavern in town. Sitting at an outside table and periodically poking his beak into a bowl of Heqet, a honey flavored beer that still survived after thousands and thousands of years, was a nondescript vulture. Effendi, agent to the criminal stars.

In his Mandarin plumage, Imperius looked equally unthreatening. Little did the other patrons of the bar know how close they were sitting to a conversation that could change their world forever.

The vulture spoke. "Dr. Drake, I presume!"

"Yes! It is I! Face to face with you at last, Effendi. All these years of conducting profitable business together and never looking each other in the eye. *(The vulture's eyes presented a nerve-wracking sight.)*

"What is so imperative that we must meet now? Have I not served your needs well and gainfully through our remote arrangement?"

"Indeed, but in this instance, the henchbeing I require must be exceptional and I wish you to be a direct part of the selection process with me. My next endeavor will outshine all of the other triumphs I have brought to fruition. Everything must be flawless, beginning with the cadre I select with your assistance. You will be well compensated."

He then began to outline the detailed specifications of background, skills, intelligence and ruthlessness needed for the job. He stressed that unquestioning compliance was crucial. No rebelliousness would be tolerated. Rewards would be beyond the imagination of the selected one but only if he, Imperius Drake, was obeyed fully and without dispute. Did such an animal exist?

Effendi squinted his eyes, raised his beak, emitted a gentle squawk and said, "Yes, I believe he does, and fortunately, he is not far away. Help yourself to a beer or whatever else you wish, and I shall make contact. I do not know his real name but he is known as The Hyena. He is quite selective about what he will do and whom he will serve. I'm glad you chose to have me participate in this process. It will be most entertaining."

Bearoness Belinda
Béarnaise Bruin
(nee Black)

# Chapter Seven

## *Polar Paradise*

*It is time for Belinda to greet*
*The Great Snake as they once again meet.*
*The Uraeus asks where*
*Is Octavius Bear?*
*But Belinda is being discreet.*

"Momma, Momma, come quick, she's back, she's back!" Arabella tugged at Belinda's leg, trying to pull her to the playroom where the Uraeus Raamjet was framed in the large screen of her game console. McTavish was seated in front of the unit, mesmerized by the cobra's glowing red eyes. Mlle Woof was dashing back and forth, trying to maintain control of the situation.

Belinda entered the room, put both of the cubs behind her and in her best bearonial demeanor bid the snake 'Good Morning.'

"Ah, the white polar consort of the Seeker of Justice and the mother of the juvenile bears." said the Uraeus, "I greet you. Am I correct that you too, are royalty?"

"Not in the strict sense! I am a Bearoness, a member of the aristocracy. This castle and all its properties are mine. My husband is a commoner but a very wealthy, powerful and intelligent commoner and I am most pleased to be his wife."

"Such an arrangement would not have been possible during the age I represent. The nobility preserved their blood lines most carefully."

"As I recall, the results were not always beneficial."

"Unfortunately, that is true. The Pharaoh whose tomb and mummy I guard was the scourge of his kingdom. It is not so much my duty to protect him from the world but to protect the world from him. Where is the Seeker of Justice? I must persuade him to take my side."

"He is with his associates. In fact, the subject of their discussion is the being whose name you uttered before you last disappeared – Imperius Drake."

"I know the name but little else. I have been warned by Anubis, the Jackal God of the Underworld that a major threat to the tranquility of the world will be brought about by this Imperius Drake and that it will involve the tomb I am bound to defend. He told me of an ursine Seeker of Justice who has defeated this Imperius in the past and ordered me to make contact with him in this manner. He is your consort?"

"Yes, he is my consort and Imperius Drake has been a life-long enemy of his and mine. We have believed several times in the past that he was killed during one of his misadventures. He seems to have a talent for survival and we believe that he has surfaced once again. We do not know what he intends but there is no doubt it will be evil and destructive. I am especially concerned for the welfare of my offspring and I personally will fight him to the death if he intends any harm to them."

"Are you convinced of my existence and credibility?"

63

"I am strongly inclined to believe that you are real but I have no way of testing your credibility. We have been subjected to arcane and subtle attacks in the past. For all I know, you may be part of the mad duck's plan."

"Duck!? Imperius Drake is a duck?"

"You didn't know? Anubis or whoever is your source told you very little, didn't he? Yes, Imperius Drake is a duck but a formidable opponent. His intelligence has few equals. He is driven with a seething hatred for all he sees as opposing him. That includes us. He has pledged revenge for all of the losses, real or imagined, he has sustained. He is a technical genius and has developed weapons beyond your comprehension. He is insane but that insanity is the engine of his cunning. Many have lived to regret calling him 'just a duck.' My consort's name is Doctor Octavius Bear. I shall persuade him and his associates to speak with you. Perhaps in several hours. Are hours familiar to you as a measurement of time?"

"Yes, but because I have lived for millennia, they mean little to me. You may have one of your children summon me on their console. I will respond."

Arabella watched the Uraeus disappear. "See, Momma, see! We told you she was real. Tell Poppa he has to listen to her. Please, Momma."

"All right, I'll talk to Poppa but I'm still not sure whether she's bad or good or what she wants from Poppa."

"She's good! She's good! We just know it, Momma!" This from McTavish.

"And now, *mes petites*," said Mlle Woof. "It is time for your language lessons."

"Can we skip language today and do ancient Egyptian history, Mademoiselle? We need to learn about King Tsk and his mummy and tomb and burial stuff. Can we?"

The Bichon looked at Belinda and got an affirmative nod. "Call Howard back at the Lair, Mlle. Doctor Bear asked him to do research on this King Tsk VI. When he's ready, we can all learn about the Pharaoh together. Yes, you two can listen in but you'll have to control yourselves. Speaking of staying under control, I suppose it's time for you to meet Inspector Wallaroo. He arrived a little earlier piloting one of my helicopters. You are absolutely forbidden to take a helicopter ride with him. He is a daredevil and will take risks that I will not tolerate. Is that understood?"

Ursine eye rolling and reluctant nods of the head. "Is That Understood? I will hear about it if you do and you *(and he)* will be sorry."

"Yes, Momma!"

"OK, let's go meet Uncle Bruce!"

Chita

# Chapter Eight

## *Polar Paradise*

*You may now give a well-mannered cheer.*
*The Octavian Team is all here.*
*Bouncing Bruce made the trek*
*And Ms. Chita's on deck.*
*Let's get on to the thing we most fear.*

Once again, the walls of Bearmoral Castle were assaulted with the sound of rotors whirling in the forecourt. The Bearoness had contracted for the installation of a traffic management and landing system in anticipation of heavy tourist and guest arrivals and departures. It wasn't completed yet and several near misses between incoming and outgoing helicopters had increased the urgency. She had also arranged for a ferry system between Unst village and the castle's dockyard. More sedate and unadventurous passengers prefer the water route. *(It's also cheaper.)*

Polar Paradise has not yet officially opened but a steady stream of early adopters are willing to put up with incomplete service and developing attractions for the sake of "being there first."

All in all, things are boding well for the new enterprise. So, it was only natural that Belinda's partner in the burgeoning venture should be arriving to survey the situation. Stepping regally out of an Aquabear executive chopper was the one, the only and the inimitable Chita, *(AKA Madame Catherine Catt)* back for another look at her investment. She is a minor partner, to be sure. Belinda and Octavius are the principal owners but she had put a substantial portion of her outsized resources on the line, partially in the resort and partially in support of a new genetics laboratory and research facility.

Dougal and two bell-dogs were at her side immediately. "Good day, Miz Chita. Welcome back to Bearmoral Castle – sorry, Polar Paradise. I'm havin' some trouble getting used to the latest name, after all the time we spent as a castle for the Bearon and his relatives. But the Bearoness, Doctor Octavius and the two bairns like the new name just fine and everyone here loves the changes. Once again, this is a fun place. Sorry, ma'am. I'm runnin' off at the mouth."

"Not at all, Dougal. I'm delighted everyone is so pleased with the place. After all, I'm a part owner and I want Polar Paradise to be a huge success. It looks like you and your staff are doing a wonderful job managing things."

"Och, Thank ye! Thank ye! We may have to add staff as the traffic builds. But first things first. We'll take your luggage to your rooms. Whom shall I call for you? Chief Inspector Wallaroo just arrived a few hours ago."

"Oh, that's a surprise. I wonder what got Brucie to cross the equator. Anyhow, I think a bowl of champagne might start things off quite well. I doubt if Octavius wants to see me but I would like to find the Bearoness, Maury and Otto. How is Otto?"

"He seems to be at the top of fitness, ma'am. He's been practicing routines with a few of the Aquabears. He's a mighty talent, he is."

"You don't know the half of it, Dougal. He saved my life. I owe him big time although in a way, I saved him as well. We're big pals. If you can find any of them, tell them I'm unwinding with a bit of bubbly in the lounge. Is Fiona still managing the bar?"

"Indeed she is, although she acts like she owns the castle. Now, we have another small white Frenchie 'chienne,' Mademoiselle Woof. She's the governess of the bairns. We're being overrun with tiny, bossy, curly haired dogs. Course, I'm a dog meself but I'm a Shetland sheep herder. That's a proper job for a canine. That was my job before I joined the castle staff. Not sure I could get a sheep to even look at me now.

"In your steward's outfit, you're bound to attract any animal's attention. OK, I'm for the bar. Thanks. See you later."

As she strode into the lounge, we bumped into each other. "Hey Short Stuff! How are you doing?"

"I've been better, Chita. Welcome back to Polar Paradise. The place is getting to look more and more like its name."

"I'm impressed. Looks like my investment will be paying off but then, just about all my investments pay off. With the exception of a late and not at all lamented Duck. What's your problem?"

"We just found out the unlamented Duck is not late."

"What?? OK. Spill it. Imperius is alive!?"

"Yeah. Bruce Wallaroo got a Black Quack delivered to him in Sydney a while back. He's just now managed to get a leave of absence"

"Oh, so that's why Brucie is here. What's the story?'

"There was nothing with the egg but the Sydney police tracked the delivery back to…ready for this? Egypt."

"Well, when's the next Aquabear shuttle to Egypt? I swore I'd kill him and I almost did. Then we all thought L. Condor sent him to a watery grave in the Ohio. Well, a cheetah's work is never done. Egypt's a big place. Any idea where he might be?"

"That's what we're trying to figure out right now. There's a lot more to the story. Finish your champagne and come join us in the twins' playroom."

"The twins' playroom? What have the cubs got do with it?"

"Look, rather than going through a whole litany of bizarre events with you, come and join the discussion. You'll know what we know in nothing flat."

"Well, you sure know how to pique a girl's interest. I assume Octavius is there."

"Of course!"

"We're not exactly lovey dovey buddies."

"Don't worry. The Bearoness has taken charge of events."

"OK, the cubs live on the second floor of the family wing, right?"

"Right!"

"See you there in a couple of minutes. You might want to warn all and sundry that I've arrived."

"The cubs will be delighted."

"Are they as cute as ever?"

"More so! They're up to their little ears in this whole thing. See you upstairs."

As I turned to head for the lift, I ran into Otto and L.Condor. "You two need to be part of this. C'mon."

"Part of what?"

"Imperius Drake is alive, well and on the loose in Egypt! Close your mouth, Otto. Sorry, Condo, you didn't kill him after all. We're heading for the cubs' playroom."

"I love the cubs, but playing with them doesn't strike me as a high priority item with that mad Duck back in action."

"Oddly enough, it does. Trust me!"

# Chapter Nine

## *Armant, Egypt*

*So Imperius gathers his crew*
*A distinctive grave robbing Who's Who!*
*For a sizeable sum,*
*They will both of them come*
*And join Bigg in his crime retinue.*

Imperius, dressed in a galibeya and fez, was just finishing his second cup of karkaday when he spotted Effendi, returning with one of the most disreputable looking animals on four feet. Not bad for a start.

Effendi fluttered and flopped over to the Duck's table, followed by the Hyena. "Let me make the introductions," squawked the vulture. "Doctor Imperius Drake, may I present Hyena. He is one of the most disreputable animals on four feet. Hyena, meet Doctor Drake, a world renowned evil genius! I have been privileged to deal with him in the past.

The spotted hyena broke into a paroxysm of laughter, sending Imperius into a full scale fit of resentment. Effendi hastened to smooth things over. "No, no, Doctor Drake! Take no offense! That is the common form of greeting of their species. In fact, I have seldom heard such enthusiasm coming from him. Clearly, you are of great interest."

"And so I should be. I am prepared to offer him an opportunity of a lifetime if he fits my highly demanding specifications. Effendi, I do not wish to have this discussion in such a public place. Where can we go to talk in secret?"

"Come with me. I have a hideout that serves many purposes. It is a mere few steps away."

A mere few steps turned out to be several miles. Since he didn't know where he was going, Imperius had to half-hop and half-fly behind the two natives, his costume fluttering and tangling his wings and talons. *(Yes, he had talons.)* He lost his fez several times. He was not pleased. They arrived at what could only be charitably described as a hovel but there was no sign of life or activity anywhere to be seen or heard. Effendi led them inside and lit several candles.

Hyena settled on his haunches and spoke for the first time in a high pitched but quite intelligible voice. "Doctor Drake! Greetings! As you will soon notice, I am quite proficient in many languages including your American English, although I am told that you are actually a Mandarin. For one assignment, I had to learn Cantonese. If you speak that language, we may be able to converse in secret when others are around. I am also capable of speaking and writing many dialects of Arabic, ranging from the common laborers' argot to the refined speech of the highly educated. You will, no doubt, require all of these in managing your enterprise."

"I am, of course, as yet uninformed about the specifics of your project but Effendi has led me to believe that tomb robbery may be involved. Without admitting to any criminal or sacrilegious activities, let me just say that many of my skills and experiences may be of great value. I have been deeply educated in Egyptology and trained in archeological techniques. I have worked in several museums and assisted in numerous digs."

"However, I have also found that the remuneration that resulted from those activities has never been satisfactory for one such as myself. It is for that reason that I have taken up somewhat irregular means of supplementing my income. Needless to say, my services do not come cheaply, but without revealing their identity, I can assure you that my clients have been more than satisfied with the results. Effendi may be able to supply you with references, should you so desire."

The Duck, somewhat taken aback for the second time, shook his head and said, "I am quite reluctant to directly communicate with anyone beyond a small group of committed parties. Perhaps, Effendi, you could produce these references without identifying who is making the request or why. Needless to say, this project could attract animals anxious to horn in on the outcome. That cannot happen and part of the work I will expect you to perform is dealing with any potential poachers. Are those skills also in your curriculum vitae?"

It was the Hyena's turn to once again be evasive. "While admitting to nothing, let us say that several situations have arisen in the past that called for somewhat extreme measures."

"All right. I shall once again trust to Effendi's judgment and recommendations. What I am about to tell you is deeply clandestine. If you choose not to participate, I will expect your total silence and I have means at my disposal to ensure that. If you do choose to participate, there must be no question of your complete dedication to the venture and to me. I will brook no deviation. You will be handsomely rewarded for your services as will Effendi, but I expect absolute and unreserved commitment. Now, what do you know about King Tsk VI?"

The hyena once again broke out in gales of "laughter" although this time it was from amazement and nervousness. "I am somewhat astonished at your target. You are aware of the Pharaoh's history and the appalling history of those who have tried to disturb his resting place."

This time Imperius laughed. "I do not intend to merely disturb his resting place. I intend to disturb him!"

# Chapter Ten

## *Polar Paradise*

*It's a hasty reunion of friends*
*Brought together to meet the same ends.*
*The mad Duck has come back*
*With his deadly Black Quack*
*And the terrible woe that portends.*

A minor mob scene had developed in the hallway outside the twins' playroom. Chita, Bruce Wallaroo, Otto, Condo, Frau Schuylkill, Colonel Where and I were milling about. Belinda, Mlle Woof and the cubs were already in the room. The only one missing from the scene was Octavius. Turns out he was finishing off a call with Howard, getting the results of the porcupine's research. Armed with a downloaded history and profile of Pharaoh Tsk VI, the Great Bear was getting prepared for his face-off with the Uraeus Raamjet.

Inside the playroom, the twins were getting antsy, asking over and over when they should try to contact Raamjet. Belinda and Mlle Woof alternately tried persuading them to be patient. Poppa needed some time to get ready for the meeting.

Belinda got an idea. "Let's go meet Uncle Bruce from Australia." Little did she know he was just outside, standing *(bouncing, springing, pacing, leaping and generally driving everyone else crazy, especially his long-time nemesis, the Frau.)*

Belinda looked at the crowd in the hall with wonderment and asked, "Are we going to talk with the Uraeus or try to overwhelm her? Bruce, Arabella and McTavish would like to meet you."

"And I'd like to meet them. Now, let's see how good a detective I am. You must be Arabella!"

"No, I'm McTavish. I have a brown spot on my left ear. See? Are you really an Inspector from Australia?"

Belinda chimed in "He's a Chief Inspector and he's very important, not only in Australia but around the world."

Arabella's eyes bugged out. "Do you have a badge? Have you worked with Poppa? Have you arrested a lot of bad guys? How did you get here from Australia? That's an awful long way to come. Why are you here?"

Bruce laughed and said, "With all those questions, I think you'd both be great detectives. Here's my badge. I flew up from Sydney and then flew one of yer Momma's helicopters from Abeardeen."

Mctavish interrupted. "You can fly a helicopter? Wow!"

Belinda looked at me and Frau Schuylkill and choked back a laugh. Bruce and choppers were subjects we had all experienced much to our severe discomfort.

The cubs grabbed each one of his forepaws. Bruce bounced and they bounced with him scattering the rest of the onlookers. Mlle Woof, who had been watching all this with some amusement, now mixed with disapproval, barked. "Ça suffit! Behave yourselves!"

The cubs laughed and let go of the Wallaroo. Bruce looked at the Bichon in shock. Could this be another Frau Schuylkill? He looked over at the Frau, who was grinning her lupine best, showing all of her teeth and shaking her head.

He had carefully avoided any mention of the reason he was here or of the history of the many scrapes he and Octavius had gone through. Let Belinda or The Bear tell them about Imperius Drake. He simply said, "Yer Poppa and I have worked together quite a bit."

Just then Octavius trundled around the corner of the corridor. Because of his size, he had to use the freight elevator *(goods lift)* to get him from floor to floor.

Belinda growled at him and asked, "Do you need all these animals to stand up to a demi-goddess cobra?"

The Bear looked at her and the entourage and said, "I'm not sure where this discussion is going to go and I want to take advantage of everyone's insight. I will introduce you all as having had experience with Imperius Drake and being able to provide useful input."

"I've been in contact with Howard and as usual, he has done an excellent job of research on the Pharaoh and his court. For your information, it seems Tsk VI was not a nice animal. He was a gigantic Hippo and was noted for his aggressive nature. His reign was relatively short but highly destructive, both within Egypt and out in the surrounding world. Many of the noble Egyptian houses were wiped out by his paranoia and fierce obsession with maintaining total control."

"He created two fearsome military units to carry out his evil whims – the Leonine Legions and the Pharaoh's Phalanx. The Phalanx was a group of elite crocodile storm troopers, sworn to support his every wish even unto their deaths, which seem to have been pretty frequent. The king perished along with most of his minions when the Imperial Barge mysteriously sank in the Nile. There did not seem to be much of a rescue effort put forth and little or no investigation of the incident ever took place. His body along with many members of the Legion and The Phalanx were recovered, mummified and buried in an unmarked tomb. There have been many archeological expeditions to find it but as far as we can tell, none have met with success. Perhaps, until now."

Chita, who had been taking this all in carefully, asked, "And now you think that crazy duck has come back from the dead, found this monster's tomb and plans to invade it. Why?"

"That's what I hope to find out. Let's go into the playroom. Arabella! You seem to have established the best connection with the Uraeus. Why don't you try to call her after we all arrange ourselves around your monitor or better yet, bring her up on McTavish's screen as well. That way we can spread out and have a better discussion."

While Arabella logged onto her station, McTavish turned to Belinda and asked, "Momma, who is this crazy duck the cheetah was talking about? Is that Imperius Drake?"

"Yes, but now you have to log on, too. You heard Poppa!"

Arabella logged on and began a search, working her way along the dark and winding tunnels of the game generated tomb. Suddenly, the surroundings changed and what was virtual became real. In a dark corner, she spied the two red lights that were the eyes of the Uraeus. She called out. "Uraeus, Raamjet, it's me, Arabella Bear! McTavish is on his console, too. Momma and Poppa are here and so are a lot of other animals who want to meet you. Please come and join us."

Slowly the bright red lights moved into the center of both screens and a reptilian face, lit by a halo-like glow, came into focus. "Ah, young ursines, you have returned. I see your noble mother is here as well. Greetings, Lady Bearoness. Is that your consort there? Yes, it is. But who are all these others?"

Belinda moved to the center of Arabella's play station. "Greetings to you, oh demi-goddess. I am pleased to see you again. Since we have last spoken, we have assembled a group of most valuable individuals. All of them have had experiences, dealings and conflicts with the despicable Imperius Drake. I will introduce them to you shortly. We are ready to trade knowledge with you and to plan how to deal with the Duck, if indeed, he is in some way threatening your mission and responsibilities."

"As you say, my consort, Doctor Octavius Bear, is by my side. He it is, the Seeker of Justice, who had been doing almost constant battle with this mad

80

criminal. We believed he was dead until we recently received convincing evidence that proves otherwise. And now, you have reason to believe he is a threat to you. Will you tell us how you came to know of him and why you feel you must seek our aid?"

Miracle of miracles, Octavius said not a word. He knew when Bel was skillfully playing a leading role and decided to leave the stage entirely to her.

Raamjet swept the group with her flaming eyes, hissed and said, "I greet you all! Are you familiar with the great jackal god, Anubis? He is the guardian and protector of the dead. It is he who presides over the ceremonies of embalming, mummification and burial. It is he who supervises the ritual of the reading of the Book of the Dead that determines the fate of the soul who is entering the Underworld. It is he who condemned the Pharaoh Tsk VI to Ammit, the goddess of retribution, along with his minions. It is he who set me the task of ensuring the buried mummy of the cursed King is never disturbed or worse yet, reanimated."

"Anubis it is, who has heard news of this Imperius Drake and his strategy to bring the Pharaoh back to life. We do not know how he will do this. We do know his intentions must be evil in the extreme and we also know he must never be allowed to succeed. We know that you, Seeker of Justice, have defeated him in the past. We require your assistance in doing so again. The god and I are not without our defensive and protective measures, if he attempts to enter our realm. We hope you can forestall him before he reaches us."

Octavius decided he had been silent long enough. "I greet you. demi-goddess and apologize for any doubt I felt toward you. You must realize how unusual your sudden appearance and now your request, must seem to us. But, our prior dealings with the Demonic Duck have taught us never to underestimate the extent of his mad schemes. If indeed he intends to revive the King, it will be a new pinnacle of insanity, even for him. We have reason to believe he is in Egypt, even as we speak. We have not yet located him precisely. I am confident we will, shortly. In fact, he may try to locate us and taunt us into coming to Egypt."

Looking at Belinda and the rest of us, he said. "And that is what I intend to do. Now, let me introduce my associates, all of whom have battled Imperius Drake. Then you must tell us how Anubis came to know about him and most important, how we may find you and the King's tomb in Egypt."

"Well, Maury," thought I, "I haven't seen a desert in quite a while. I've never seen a Uraeus or a Pharaoh's tomb. AND I'm really looking forward to seeing how the Great Bear handles the Sahara heat. What I'm not looking forward to is crossing swords again with, as Frau Schuylkill calls him, that *verdammt duck.*"

# Chapter Eleven

## *Armant, Egypt*

*The mad Drake starts by sharing his plan*
*To revive the lost King, if he can.*
*He will bring back to life*
*That great agent of strife.*
*The royal scourge of a most evil clan.*

It was difficult to tell who was more amazed, Effendi or Hyena. The vulture spoke first. "Do I understand correctly, Doctor Drake, that you plan to raise the Pharaoh from the dead?"

Imperius chortled. "Quite astute of you, my neophron friend. That is exactly what I intend to do. I have discovered that the Egyptian process for mummification is reversible in many instances. Depending on how the process was originally carried out, the spirit of the deceased can be called back from the Underworld, which is no more, no less than an alternate universe. My research in the case of King Tsk VI leads me to believe that he and his followers were sent to their resting place through a rather hasty and possibly incomplete procedure."

"The Pharaoh and his minions perished in a mysterious sinking of the Royal Barge in the flooding Nile. Most of the bodies were recovered but before any investigations could be launched, if any were indeed intended, their bodies were hastily mummified or disposed of and their spirits hurriedly committed to the nether world. Corners were cut in the process and I wish to recover the Book of the Dead that facilitated the procedures. At the moment, this book is under the watchful eye of a Uraeus named Raamjet. She must be eliminated. I have the resources to do that but I must rely on you, Hyena, to find the burial site and once we have the Book, act as interpreter for me. Once I have reached full understanding of the necessary conditions that must be met, I will reinstate the King into an active and conscious state."

"He will then be the catalyst for my plan to conquer the cosmos."

Hyena, giggling softly to himself, wondered what kind of a nut he was listening to. He was well acquainted with the Pharaonic legends and the stories of mysterious efforts to communicate with dead royalty but this was sheer madness.

"Doctor Drake, you will perhaps pardon me if I point out that others have tried projects like what you are proposing and have met with complete and expensive failure."

"I will pardon you, Hyena, only because you have no knowledge of my brilliance and Type AAA personality. In this case, failure will not be an option. *(Where had Hyena and Effendi heard that before?)* Now, let us be clear about what I am offering you. In addition to very substantial payment for your services, you will be participating in an event and process that will quite literally, totally change this world and others forever. You will be let in on the underground floor so to speak. *(The Duck's sense of humor ran to the bizarre.)* If you choose not to participate in this venture, I will have to treat you as a potential threat, since you already know too much of my intent. The same applies to you, Effendi."

Both the vulture and hyena took serious umbrage at this and spontaneously attacked the Duck. Alas, they were not aware of the Black Quack, the same device that he had recently sent to Bruce Wallaroo and had used in many of his previous forays against Octavius Bear. It was the same device that originally brought Chita and Bigg Baboon to their knees in the African wilds in Book One - *The Open and Shut Case*.

The Black Quack is an egg shaped apparatus that emits an ear piercing, debilitating sound that can destroy the hearing, balance and ultimately, the sanity of those exposed to it. The device, which is telekinetically controlled by Imperius Drake, resists all attempts to destroy or disable it. Needless to say, Effendi and Hyena were rapidly subdued and lost all desire to further assault Imperius. The Duck shut the Black Quack down.

Hyena asked the same question that every victim comes up with. "What is that thing?"

Imperius, his ego at maximum strength, replied. "That, my friend, is the Black Quack and I alone control it. It has driven many of my enemies to lunacy. I would prefer not to inflict that on either of you but I *will* be obeyed and I *will not* countenance threats. Take it as an example of my superior technical and scientific capability. Have no doubts, gentlebeasts! I can carry out what I claim. King Tsk VI and his followers will be reanimated and I will then clone these immortals to create the most formidable army the world has ever seen. Imperius Drake will indeed be Imperial!! Now shall we take it as agreed that you will be working for me and with me in this colossal venture?"

The vulture and hyena nodded their heads but with serious mental reservation. This duck was indeed a loon and after they had completed their assignments, they were certain he would seek out ways of eliminating them. They must beat him to the punch. But for the nonce, their curiosity had been tweaked and they decided they would play along.

Hyena spoke, "All right, Duck, what are your orders?"

"You will henceforth refer to me as 'Sire.' You will accompany me back to my island hideaway where you will meet my assistant, Bigg Baboon. There I will outline my cunning plan to all of you."

"Now, let us end this meeting on a high note. When we reach the island, you will find comfortable quarters, a sumptuous supply of food and drink and 100,000 Euros in cash for each of you as an opening payment for your services. There will be more as the project moves forward. Effendi, I believe you will be needed only during the planning and outfitting stages where your knowledge and connections will be of great value. Once we reach the actual process of implementation, I expect Hyena to carry the burden. Now, Effendi, please arrange transportation for us back to the coast. We have much to do."

*(Imperius has neatly avoided any mention of the challenge he had thrown down to Bruce Wallaroo and hence, to Octavius Bear. He knew that sending a Black Quack to that ridiculous Australian would stir the Bear and his underlings to action. They would know the egg had come from Egypt and would move in this direction. His hatred for that odious ursine knew no bounds. He had an overpowering desire to settle scores permanently but first*

*he would demonstrate his brilliance with this wonderful coup. He also wanted a chance to deal with Chita and the Andean Condor who had almost killed him over the Ohio River. He would reserve those intentions to himself for the moment.)*

# Chapter Twelve

## *Polar Paradise*

*Raamjet's story has struck a strong key*
*And the team is quite eager to see*
*That the infamous Duck*
*Has a streak of bad luck*
*And gets beaten as quick as can be.*

After all and sundry had been introduced to Raamjet, she proceeded to tell us about Anubis and how he learned of the plots and plans of Imperius Drake. The Duck had appeared almost a year ago on a nondescript island in the Red Sea and had proceeded to set up a laboratory and living quarters. He also acquired a boat from a local fishercat but he didn't seem able to operate it himself. He has an assistant of some sort, a Baboon, who also seemed to be pretty hopeless in sailing and navigation.

The fishercat became suspicious of what these interlopers were going to do when he heard the Baboon and Duck talking to each other about tombs and mummies and ancient kings. The fishercat is a faithful believer in the ancient ways and prayed to Anubis to warn him of these interlopers. The god, in turn, appeared to the fishercat in a dream, thanked him for the warning and proceeded to search out the Duck and Baboon. Unable to physically deal with them, he could explore their minds and souls. What he learned was beyond belief. They planned to reanimate the Pharaoh Tsk VI, his Phalanx and the Leonine Legions and use them for world conquest. They must be stopped. It was then he also warned the Uraeus, Raamjet.

Together, from the Underworld, Anubis and Raamjet could control the spirit of Tsk VI. But they needed physical assistance in the world above in actively pursuing and thwarting this mad Anatid. He must be prevented from tomb invasion, mummy sacrilege and any attempt to reanimate the cursed king. They sought the help of Osiris, Lord of the Underworld. He told them of Octavius Bear, the Seeker of Justice, and his continued struggles with Imperius Drake.

It was left to Raamjet, the Uraeus, to contact Octavius. She did, through the cubs, and our story picks up from there.

"So, Tavi, are you convinced that nutty Duck is at it again?"

"Unfortunately, Bel, I am. Raamjet has given us a pretty good idea of where he is holed up. I'm sorry to put this on highest priority but you all know what a threat Imperius is. I haven't the slightest idea of how he is going to pull this off. I'm not even sure of why he wants to do this."

Chita spoke up. "As he goes on, that serum he takes is making him more of a menace. Cosmic domination through reanimated Egyptian armies is just the kind of screwy thing only he is capable of coming up with. When I was with him, he had serious delusions of grandeur. Now, he's off the charts. Octavius, I still have a score to settle with him. I want in on this project."

The Great Bear paused, blew out his cheeks and said, "You know I have a lot of issues with you, Chita. But of all of us, you've probably got the most experience with Imperius. HOWEVER, I will not stand for any wild solo vendettas that could scuttle our efforts."

89

The Colonel looked at Frau Ilse, Condo and me and said, "Well, we're about to embark on a real multiverse experience. I assume you all realize that this Underworld may turn out to be the best example yet of a parallel universe. It might be this crazy duck is doing us a favor. I think we need to get Howard in on this ASAP."

Octavius was listening in and said, "Good thinking, Colonel. He's probably way ahead of us. I'll contact him. *(Just what Howard needed!)* Meanwhile, will you and the Frau get started on setting up an Egyptian campaign. The Ursa Major is housed in Abeardeen and ready to go, isn't it? The C-5A is suited to desert travel and we'll need lots of cargo space. We'll have to get our paws on several large vehicles suitable for desert travel. We'll also need some major air conditioning and climate suits for those of us unaccustomed to the heat of arid regions. Maury, you'll finally get a chance to get back to your typical boyhood weather. Is the Sahara's climate the same as the Kalahari's?"

"I don't know, Octavius, but I'm willing to chance it."

"All right. Let's organize. Who goes and who stays here? Bel, I think you, Mlle Woof and the cubs should remain for the time being, at least. We need to keep contact with Raamjet and as long as she is communicating through the cubs' play stations, we'll need you here. Senhor Condor! Can you rig up a relay system from the play stations so we can communicate with the Uraeus as we travel?"

"Easy to do, Doctor Bear. I'll see what I can do to create a direct link with her once we're in Egypt."

"Are you up for joining us, Inspector?"

"Do you think I'd miss an opportunity to tangle with that flaky Duck and his no-good Baboon. After all, he sent his blistering noise maker to me."

"Good! It looks like the expedition will consist of the Inspector, Maury, Otto, Colonel Where, Frau Schuylkill, Senhor Condor, Chita and myself."

The cubs were already besieging Belinda with whimpering entreaties to go along. "Please Momma, we've never been to Egypt. We've never been anywhere except here. We're the ones the Uraeus talks to. We discovered her. She'll want to meet us."

Belinda wanted to keep thousands of miles between Imperius Drake and her offspring. "Let's let Poppa and his team get set up in Egypt and then we'll see what we can do.  You're needed here to help keep contact with Raamjet. That's very important!"

Mlle Woof intervened. "It is time for lunch, mes petits. Then, we will download some apps and material about ancient and modern Egypt and become extra smart about all the gods and monuments and mummies and tombs and hieroglyphs."

"What are hyraglifs?"

"They're picture writing that the ancient Egyptians used – not at all like the way we write. Come! You'll see!"

# Chapter Thirteen

## *A Nondescript Island in the Red Sea*

*In a tomb built with great ancient stones*
*Lies the Pharaoh, his skin and his bones.*
*And in chambers nearby*
*His fierce armies all lie.*
*These the Duck wants to turn into clones.*

"Hieroglyphs! Hieroglyphs! That is where you will be of greatest value to me, Hyena. We must be able to read the Pharaoh's Book of the Dead. You must translate it with unerring accuracy. It is only by tracing the processes defined in that scroll that we will be able to reach and re-animate the King."

Imperius was in another one of his turbocharged rants. After making brief stops to pick up essentials, they had reached the island. Following introductions to Bigg Baboon, the four of them were seated in a circle, prepared for a discussion. What they didn't realize, and Bigg knew only too well, is that Imperius' version of a discussion is listening to Imperius.

So far, he had told them a half accurate, half wildly inventive tale of the death of the Pharaoh. Unfortunately, none of his listeners could determine what was fact and what was fiction. Clearly, the Duck believed it was all true. He also believed he knew the rough whereabouts of the King's burial place, although he refused to reveal his sources. Not for Tsk VI was the Valley of the Kings. No, he was buried somewhere in the western desert away from Thebes and far from the Nile that had taken his life. Probably entombed to the south of the Temple of Amun in Siwa. This was to be the great task entrusted to Effendi and Hyena. Find the tomb!

This was not the first time that Effendi had been involved in a search for King Tsk's burial site. There had been several other expeditions mounted in recent years. All failed. One, however, seemed to be getting close when the money ran out. In fact, he was reasonably sure he knew where the tomb was within a few kilometers. Ground penetrating radar (GPR) was needed to confirm his suppositions. But, he was not about to suggest any of this to Imperius until a few operating ground rules were firmly established.

First, and probably most important, neither of them trusted the Duck to keep his part in the bargain. This called for significant payment in advance. It also called for his major investment in equipment and labor. Would Imperius open the project to outside labor? His paranoia suggested that he wouldn't. This would slow the project to a crawl. How would they remove all the earth and stone surrounding the tomb? *(Readers of previous volumes of these Casebooks may have an inkling on how the Duck planned to pull off that Herculean task.)* But the most important issue was preventing Imperius from attempting to do away with them once the Pharaoh was found and re-animated. Just how did the mad scientist plan to pull off that miracle? They needed to know more.

And who was this Baboon? Bigg? Was that his name? He said little and Imperius treated him as if he was a brainless underling. Probably suited for heavy duty work and little more. Strangely, in Egyptian history and culture, baboons were closely associated with Thoth, the god of wisdom, science and measurement. They kept the scales that weighed the heart of the deceased in the judgment of the dead. Baboons also guarded the first gate of the underworld. Did Imperius know any of this? Was Bigg Baboon to be an important player in this expedition? Did Bigg know any of this? Again, Effendi would hold this information to himself until the proper time came, if ever. Time now to curtail the Duck's monologue and get down to negotiations. Let's work on his limitless ego.

"Doctor Drake, Hyena and I are indeed enthralled by the breathtaking audacity of your proposal. Others have tried to uncover the tomb of Tsk VI but none had dared to consider actually bringing the Pharaoh back to life. You are clearly a genius of unique foresight and vision. But there are a few things that are dampening our enthusiasm, especially since you have already threatened us. While your infernal black egg is a fearsome device, it is as nothing compared to the vengeance the ancient gods of Egypt could wreak upon us all, here and in the afterlife. I am afraid that we must know more of your plans in detail before we agree to risk our fate with you. Oh, and we will not call you 'Sire' and we will be treated as equals."

Once again, Imperius was taken aback. First Bigg was showing signs of resistance and now these two insisted on exercising what they believed to be their rights. Well, he would play along with them. In truth, finding new co-conspirators would be a time consuming nuisance. But, he would watch them and remember. Yes, he would remember.

"Perhaps you are not aware that I am the world's greatest geneticist. I have carried out highly sophisticated experiments, and established new and mind numbing principles and methods that some would see as magic rather than science. I can assure you that, through the application of genetic

94

disciplines, it is possible to reverse the physical effects of death, and even the process of mummification."

"The resulting beings will not be totally independent and sentient. Rather, and this is most important to my plans, they will be robust, mobile, rational, communicative individuals who lack any form of will power. They will be mine and only mine, to command. Then, by an equally amazing process, I will clone these individuals into a vast army of lions and crocodiles that will dominate the world. All under my command! Even the Hippopotamus King. Mine to dictate! In the cosmic conflict, some will, no doubt, be destroyed, but I will have an endless supply of replacements."

The thought of a mere Duck dominating these fearful creatures left Effendi and Hyena doubtful, to say the least. Imperius sensed their uncertainty.

"These are not wild suppositions. These are facts, borne out in my laboratories. Bigg Baboon will attest to the success of my experiments."

For the first time, the Baboon spoke up. "What he says is true. He's done it. There were early failures but the Emperor has succeeded." *(And frightened the hell out of him in the process. Bigg has been plotting how he would get away from the loony duck for some time now. The presence of these two might be his ticket to freedom. What he would do with his new freedom was a puzzle, but he would try.*

# Chapter Fourteen

## *Polar Paradise*

*We start off with our massive campaign*
*"Stop the Duck who is clearly insane!"*
*Making contacts galore,*
*Loading weapons and more*
*In the hold of Octavius' plane.*

Colonel Where looked over at Octavius and said, "We have a bit of strategizing to do. First off, how do we explain to the Egyptian government, their police and their Department of Antiquities why we want to fly in a C-5A loaded with equipment and personnel? Do we want to make them aware of what we believe Imperius is up to? Perhaps Inspector Wallaroo is the best individual to make contact. International law enforcement and all that. Do you have any contacts there, Bruce?"

"During my days with the Interpol Fine Arts and Jewelry Protective Squad, I had dealings with the Interior Minister as well as the Tourism and Antiquities Police, especially a Major Akil. He's a cat, an Egyptian Mau. Fast on his feet and smart. Spotted, too. Remind you of anyone, Chita? Any road, we owe each other a few favors. How much of the story do you want me to tell him?"

Octavius pawsed for a moment and said, "Let's just present it as a case of potential tomb robbery. That's all we know for sure, anyway. Our interest in Imperius Drake goes back a good way, and he is wanted internationally for a number of crimes. He destroyed a priceless jewel. He has personally assaulted several of our group and we, in turn, have had a few near misses with him. We will play by the government's rules, but we believe we are in the best position to deal with this menace. Stress how, in the past, we have assisted many other governments in the pursuit of criminals and in preventing major felonies. I'm sure the U.S. authorities as well as Shetland Yard would be willing to speak on our behalf."

"Ocko, I wouldn't be the least bit surprised if Major Akil and the Antiquities Police are well acquainted with you. I'll give him a shout right now."

"Thanks Inspector! Good thinking, Colonel. Now, has anyone else had experience with ancient Egyptian artifacts or traditions?"

"In fact, Octavius, I do," purred Chita, "from my days in Paris. I know Akil, and in spite of *(or maybe because of)* my bad girl reputation, we got on quite well. I never got to Cairo, but he was often in Europe attending conferences. I can't remember, but he may already be aware of Imperius. I don't think I ever introduced the two of them. The Duck avoided the police as often as he could. I had no problem with an Egyptian policeman."

"Egypt does have an extradition agreement with the United States, Chita or should I call you Madame Catherine Catt"

"Thanks for the information, Maury. They have one with England, too where I'm currently residing. I'm not bothered. And the Catherine Catt alias has often come in handy, I'll have you know."

We hadn't heard from Otto for a while. "Hey, Mr. Magnificent, are you up for another round with Imperius and Bigg?"

"You bet. I owe him big time for his attempts to turn me into a slave. He may have done me a favor activating some of my adrenaline based capers, but I'm still not sure if I'm going to turn into a complete nut case, courtesy of his serum. Besides, I can probably zap around a tomb more easily than any of you."

Octavius took this as an opportunity to poll the group. "If any of you are dubious and want out of this expedition, now is the time to speak up."

No comments!

"OK, let's get organized. Frau Schuylkill and Colonel, can you go to Abeardeen and get the Ursa Major fitted up for desert duty including some added refrigeration and weapons? Once again, we may have to smuggle the Particle Beam Accelerators in under false pretenses. But I'm afraid we'll need those weapons. I'm willing to bet heavily that Imperius wouldn't have set out on this campaign without having built replacements for the ones we destroyed. He may even have improved on the design. One of the features of that device is moving or disintegrating large objects like sand dunes, boulders and walls. Otherwise, after he found the site, he would have to hire a large team of laborers to dig out the entrance and passageways. That's not the Duck's style. He may try to kill the Uraeus. She needs to be warned, although she seems quite formidable in her own right. I don't think I'd like to mix it up with those eyes and fangs."

"Senhor Condor, what have we got or what can we get in the electronic search department?"

"Once we have a clearer picture from the Uraeus of where it is generally located, we will have to rent time on infra-red satellites to precisely scan for the tomb. We should also get our claws on a Ground Penetrating Radar rig mounted on a drone. We can make limited use of infra-red communication as well as wireless. We may be able to set up some wireless underground nodes but that will take some intense logistics. I'll get on it immediately. We will probably have to use a couple of the estate's helicopters to go on shopping tours."

"Fine, but time is of the essence. We don't know how far along Imperius is or how well he has thought this all out. We're not even sure of what his final objective is. I can't imagine that he and Bigg Baboon are going to be the only players. In fact, do we even know if the Baboon is still with him? Maury and Inspector Wallaroo, we need to know where he is at the moment and who is with him. Can you tackle that?"

Chita interrupted. "Why don't Bruce and I follow up on that with Major Akil? We should also backtrack that Black Quack he shipped to you in Sydney, Bruce. Maury and Otto ought to follow up on that fishercat that Raamjet mentioned. He probably can identify his boat and tell us where they might be. It may be time for us to get back in touch with the Uraeus. We could use some more input from her."

Octavius grudgingly agreed. Chita may have a criminal history but she is damn smart. Often too damn smart.

Back in the playroom, Belinda and Mlle Woof watched as the cubs logged on to the Tomb Raider game and tried to call up the Uraeus. The Great Bear had called Belinda and asked her to get as much information as she could about the location, layout, disposition and condition of the Pharaoh's tomb.

"Raamjet, Raamjet, it's us! Arabella and McTavish. We're here with Momma and Mlle Woof. Momma needs to talk to you. Please come!"

Two glowing red disks approached the screen. "I greet you, children of the noble Bearoness. I will speak with her. I greet you, too, little white protector of the cubs. Are you teaching them about the glories of ancient Egypt? There is much for them to learn."

Mlle Woof had only spoken to the snake once before. She stared at the screens, barked hesitantly and replied, "I am teaching them such as I know and such as we can glean from Internet sources. Are you aware of the Internet?"

"My powers as a demi-goddess provide me with the means to intercept your transmissions. That is how I communicate with you now. I have no devices. I need no devices."

Belinda moved in front of the screens. "I greet you, Uraeus. I have much to tell you and I have many things I need to ask. Shall we begin?"

"I find your efficiency refreshing. For too long I have been subjected to the useless formalities of ceremony and pomp. Say what you will."

Belinda proceeded to tell her that Octavius was mounting an expedition to go to the tomb and disrupt the strategy of Imperius Drake. They were also seeking him out at that very moment before he reached the tomb. It was uncertain whether he knows the location of the burial place or not. They believe he is currently on an island in the Red Sea. It is unclear what his specific plans are but he has been known to mount complex, even preposterous efforts. Simplicity was not his style. He, no doubt, also had at his disposal sophisticated weapons and devices for uncovering and entering the mausoleum. It is also unknown who is assisting him.

They were trying to locate the fishercat who had sold or rented his boat to them. If Raamjet could identify him, it would be most helpful. But most important for the moment, is getting a precise location of the tomb and the King's mummy.

The Uraeus gave a surprising reply. "I do not know exactly where the tomb is in your terms. I exist in a half way state between the Underworld and your Upperworld. Your dimensions and mine are not the same. I do know that the burial was done in a hastily built mastaba in the desert far to the west of the Nile. It is here that the mummy rests. Does the name Siwa still have meaning?"

"Yes, it does. Is that where the site is?"

"No, but that is where the procession of priests and officials took up residence while the mummification of the King and his armies took place. They did not want to have his body resting in a known place. Siwa was a staging area. I was called up from the Underworld by Osiris and Anubis to

101

take up my station once the tomb and mummification was completed. And here I remain."

"I shall summon the fishercat who prayed to Anubis and learn his name and location. I shall ask where the Duck took his boat. You may also meet the fishercat when you get to Egypt."

"That would be most helpful. One of our number is a condor, a bird of huge size. He is also an expert on telecommunication. He will be constructing devices our team can use to contact you wherever they are. You will no longer need to talk to us through the play stations."

This set the twins off. "Momma, we want to keep talking to Raamjet. Don't let Condo disconnect us. Please, Momma!"

The Uraeus answered them. "I shall keep in contact with you, young bears. Do not fear. You have been a great help to me and to your friends. I shall not forget you."

Belinda said, "See! You have nothing to worry about. Condo will not disconnect you."

"Momma, why can't we go with Poppa to Egypt? You and Mlle Woof can come along. We'll behave. There'll be plenty of room for us in the plane."

The Bichon interrupted. "Little ones, what your Poppa is going to be doing will be very dangerous. We all want you to be safe here in the castle."

"Momma, aren't you going with Poppa? He'll need you!"

This same thought had been troubling Belinda. She wanted to be with Octavius. She had been on several dangerous excursions with the Great Bear in the past and had been more than helpful. Besides, Imperius Drake had come close to killing her. No one does that to Bearoness Belinda Béarnaise Bruin Bear (nee Black.) She thought the Duck had been killed in a mid air collision with Condo. It seems she and everyone else was wrong. Well, if at first you don't succeed... She must have a discussion with Octavius and quickly.

# Chapter Fifteen

## *Still Polar Paradise*

*Time to summon up Major Akil*
*And to make an approval appeal.*
*He's the Police Commandant.*
*With his government's grant*
*Our excursion will be a done deal*

Chita and Bruce called over to Condo. "Join us. We're going to try to reach Major Akil. Your knowledge of the technology might come in handy during the conversation."

The condor nodded and hopped out after them. They moved toward one of the rooms that Octavius had set up as a general purpose headquarters, complete with computing, telecommunications and display facilities. The Great Bear also had a room devoted to UUI business. Both were super secure.

"Oh damn, we need passwords and visual ID."

The bird touched his voice generator and spoke to Octavius. Chita and Bruce stared at him, wondering what he had just done.

"The Frau and Colonel are on their way," he said in a voice that sounded for all the world, like the Great Bear.

"How do you do that, Condo?"

"The wonders of UUI technology. While we were designing my voice generator, we decided to throw in some additional features. As you know, I have no voice box of my own. I am naturally mute. This changes all that."

He pointed to a small unit attached to his neck. We're working on a subcutaneous version, but this one is quite powerful and versatile. I can throw my voice for hundreds of feet. I can switch back and forth among vocal characteristics and mimic just about anyone's tones and accents. We just added some telephony to the mix. I just thought about Octavius and the device automatically called him. I hear him through bone conduction."

The two wolves had arrived. Between them, they designed, implemented, maintained and upgraded on an almost constant basis, the security of the Bear's Lair in Cincinnati, Polar Paradise in the Shetlands, and his aircraft and vehicles The colonel handed chip cards to Condo and Chita.

"Use these to open doors, boot up equipment and log onto apps. We change the codes at random short intervals. You may also have to pass a retinal scan. We have you on record from your previous visits. Go ahead and give it a try."

Chita took the card, held it against the door lock and was immediately challenged. The lock wanted her name and retinal scan. She typed 'Chita' into the keyboard and peered into a lens. The door clicked and started to open but immediately went into challenge mode again because of the others. Each had to go through the same process. Finally, it swung wide and allowed the four of them to go into the room.

The Frau opened up a communications channel and Inspector Wallaroo connected his UUI Clever Phone with its address book to the system. One ring and a spotted cat in military uniform came on the line.

"Akil here!"

"G'day Major. Chief Inspector Bruce Wallaroo here. Hopin' you remember me from some of our previous ventures."

"Inspector Bruce or is it now Chief Inspector? Of course, I remember you. I still have a broken chair in my office to remind me."

Chita ambled over, peered into screen and said, "Hello Major! Remember me?"

"Madame Catt, is it not? Well this is indeed an unexpected surprise. What brings you two to call upon a humble antiques policeman? Dare I believe that this call is more than social?"

"Sorry to say we have some business we'd like to do with you, Major," said the Inspector, "We have reason to believe that a tomb robbery is being planned by an old time nemesis of ours, Imperius Drake."

"I am well aware of Imperius Drake. I am not aware of any attempt of tomb robbery, however. How do you know of this?"

"We have heard from several anonymous sources that he is in Egypt and making his plans. We thought he was dead but no such bloomin' luck. We understand that he is planning to search for the tomb of Pharaoh Tsk VI."

106

"I am sorry, Chief Inspector, but the location of that tomb has never been discovered. Our best guess is that if it exists at all, it would be somewhere in the western desert. There are a few fragments of historical records that speak of it but King Tsk VI was regarded as a deadly tyrant and his death went unmourned. It is not even certain if he was ever mummified."

Chita replied, "To tell you the truth, Major, we are less concerned about finding the King's tomb as we are capturing Imperius Drake. He is a true menace and needs to be put out of business, once and for all. We have the team to do it."

"Unfortunately, Madame Catt, I lack the resources or justification to pursue him myself, unless it can be proven that he is planning, and will be engaged in the robbery of a tomb that may not even exist."

Bruce said, "All we want at the moment is your government's permission to fly a suitably equipped aircraft into the desert and search out his whereabouts. We fully understand that this is your jurisdiction and we will obey Egyptian laws and keep you totally informed. We are currently based in the Shetland Islands but we have the ability to fly nonstop to Egypt. Our team will include eight persons, each of whom has knowledge and experience with Imperius Drake. It will be led by no less than the famous Octavius Bear."

Akil replied, "I am familiar with Doctor Bear. He has made a number of generous donations to help restore several of our temples. Give me twenty-four hours and I will have an answer for you. I will also want to be personally involved as your plans unfold. I must keep my superiors satisfied that this effort is justified. Meanwhile, I would appreciate a document outlining Imperius Drake's history that I can present to them."

Bruce looked at Chita. "You've had the most experience with him. Feel up to a little literary work?"

The Cat half smiled and half snarled. "OK, I'll try to keep it believable but it won't be easy. I'll be back to you in a few hours, Major. I warn you. This guy is a true loony. I hope your superiors have a good sense of the preposterous. But be warned, he is indeed a serious threat. He came within seconds of annihilating a thousand genetic scientists."

The Major looked at the two of them and said, "When you deal in Egyptian antiquities, nothing is unbelievable. While you're making the case, I will contact my superiors at the Ministry. But let me warn *you*. We do not take kindly to having our time wasted."

The Wallaroo replied, "That's why we'll be doing the heavy lifting. We just want your okey-dokey to get going. By the way, let's keep this as secret as possible."

Chita thought to herself. "We're gonna land a big-ass airplane in the middle of the desert complete with a team of eight high powered animals and he wants to keep it secret. Oh, Brucie, you are too much."

# Chapter Sixteen

## *A Nondescript Island in the Red Sea*

*Imperius unfolds his plan.*
*They must start up as soon as they can.*
*With his marvelous gun*
*He will not be outdone.*
*Yes, it's time his great venture began!*

Imperius looked at the trio and said, "I have carefully researched the history and characteristics of King Tsk VI and I am convinced that, through the application of my impeccable logic and vast knowledge, I can discern where and under what circumstances he is buried. There is probably a Uraeus guarding his crypt but that should be no matter to us."

Neither Effendi nor Hyena liked the sound of that. Bigg, as usual, was clueless. "What's a Uraser?"

"Uraeus, Uraeus! It is a large cobra-like snake that spits venom from its fangs and shoots fire from its eyes. It is a demi-god or goddess who answers to the god Anubis. But certainly no problem for us and our endoatmospheric particle beam projector."

Both Effendi and Hyena reacted. "Your what?"

Bigg cut in, "It's a laser powered ray gun. I'm in charge *(a baboon pun)* of it. It can knock over a building or drill a hole thinner than a hyena hair. It's a real weapon."

Imperius added, "It will also be used to dig our way into the mastaba once we locate it with ground penetrating radar. No heavy digging equipment. No swarms of workers."

Effendi asked, "Where do you expect to acquire ground penetrating radar equipment?"

"That, my dear Effendi, will be one of your first assignments after we come to terms. Now, gentlebeasts, are we agreed that you will be eager and energetic participants in this wonderful enterprise?"

A lengthy silence.

"Come, come," said the Duck, hitching up his galibeya for about the hundredth time, "how often will an opportunity such as this come your way?"

The vulture wasn't sure he ever wanted an opportunity like this to come his way and the hyena also looked doubtful. However, the prospect of major treasure and monies struck them both. Greed overcame fear *(and good sense.)*

They reluctantly agreed and were presented with a significant amount of cash.

"Now," said Imperius, "we must plan out the program, establish logistics, make assignments and further study the known information about the

Pharaoh and his court. I shall make a special inquiry into the nature and vulnerabilities of the Uraeus. You, Hyena, will serve as my translator and researcher. I must have totally reliable facts with which to plan and execute this campaign."

"You, Bigg, must work with and further refine your use of the particle projector. It is crucial to our success."

Bigg, who at this point, was getting increasingly annoyed at the entire proceeding grudgingly nodded his head. He was getting less and less enthused about this whole caper. He had always believed, as Chita had told him so many times, that Imperius had gone completely off his trolley. Now, he was certain. He needed to figure out how to break away from the Duck without being subjected to the deadly Black Quack.

*****

Back at the Bear's Lair, Howard Watt had turned from his work on the Multiverse Project to pursue another avenue that had been gnawing at him ever since he heard that Imperius and probably Bigg, was still alive. If they were back in business, they probably had another copy of the endoatmospheric particle projector. If, as Octavius told him, Imperius was engaged in an operation of tomb robbery, what better tool than the ray gun for making short work of the mastaba and its surroundings. As they all knew, it was also an extremely deadly weapon. He needed to talk with Octavius, the Colonel and Condo…and now!

# Chapter Seventeen

## *Polar Paradise and Abeardeen Airport*

*How do bears deal with stark desert heat?*
*Can they stand it without getting beat?*
*We'll find out soon enough*
*When the going gets tough.*
*The Great Bear won't accept a defeat.*

At that particular moment, Octavius, the Colonel, Frau Schuylkill, Condo, Chita, Bruce, Otto and I were working up assignments and a checklist of items and activities necessary before heading for the desert.

"Ach," said the Frau, "A Kodiak bear in the Sahara Desert! I wonder if the Bearoness intends to go, too. A polar bear in the Sahara!"

Octavius rumbled. "I'm not looking forward to it. We need some refrigerator suits. And no, Bel will not be coming along. She's staying here with the cubs." *(Little did he know.)*

"How about us?" the Colonel replied, "Wolves aren't exactly desert creatures, either."

I piped up, "For the first time since I signed up with you, Octavius, I will be going where a meerkat belongs. The Sahara outclasses the Kalihari but what the hell."

"Hell is exactly right, Maury," Condo remarked. "All that hot air will make it nearly impossible from me to take off."

"It won't be easy for the Ursa Major, either but I think the engines are up to it." said the Colonel. "Ilse, we need to get down to Abeardeen in a hurry."

Octavius intervened. "I've got Howard on the phone and he wants to talk to all of us. Hold on while we bring him up on video."

A twitching nose and beady eyes surrounded by a halo of spines appeared on the screens. "Hi, Shetlands. How goes it?"

"Busy, Howard. Imperius is at it again."

"I know! That's what I wanted to talk to you about. If he plans to unearth an Egyptian tomb with the smallest possible crew, he's going to use the endoatmospheric weapon. That gun can move earth, destroy stone, dig holes and oh, yes, kill. I'll bet he has another one or two of them at his disposal. I'll also bet he's made some enhancements. He's been in love with that thing since he first swiped one from the UUI labs. If he means to reach the mummy, he's not going to be too conscientious about leaving the rest of the tomb intact."

"He's also going to want a GPR unit – Ground Penetrating Radar. If Bigg is still with him, the baboon can certainly handle the ray gun. We've seen him do it. But I don't know about the GPR. Imperius is too much of a prima donna to take on a task like that, himself. He's going to require expert help. You'd better follow that trail pretty quickly. I'm sure there are GPR services in

113

Egypt, strictly on the basis of archeological research. There are aerial services and ground based units. He'll need both."

"Have you made up your mind whether you want to cut him off at the pass or follow him when and if he's uncovered the tomb?"

Octavius replied, "Ideally, we'd like to just let sleeping kings lie. I want to take the preventive route but it may already be too late for that. As far as we know, he and his cohorts, whoever they are, are holed up on an island in the Red Sea. A fishercat sold or rented them his boat or so we are told by Raamjet, the tomb's guardian Uraeus. We need to find that cat. I'm sending Maury, Otto and Senhor Condor on ahead of us to search him out and check out the GPR services."

*(This was big news for Maury, Otto and Condo. Octavius simply believes that "wishing will make it so." However, after being with the Great Bear for years, you learn to adapt, anticipate and, in my case, obey. Otto and Condo weren't at that stage yet but I am. Start packing. I guess we can take the Bearoness' Aquabear SST to Cairo. She has a new flight crew to replace Bearnice and Bearyl who are now embroiled in show biz and are two of my agency clients. I haven't met the new cockpit team yet but no doubt I will, very shortly.)*

Several hours later, a large utility copter swung away from the Polar Paradise pad and headed south for Abeardeen airport. At the controls were the Colonel and Frau, on their way to fit up the Ursa Major for the "invasion" of Egypt. Also on board: Otto, Condo and me *(or is it "I.")* We're on our way to board the Aquabear SST for our trip to Cairo as an advanced party.

114

Mission: Locate Imperius and his group and if possible, stop him before he gets started. At a minimum find out what the hell he is up to. We know he wants to discover and unearth the mummy of Tsk VI but for what reason? Knowing him, he probably has yet another harebrained criminal scheme under his wing. They keep getting more and more spectacular. As if trying to kill off a thousand geneticists and attempting to destroy UUI and the Bear's Lair with Octavius in it isn't enough for one lifetime. This one will, no doubt, be a beauty. Oh well, life is never dull when you work for a Great Bear who seems to attract homicidal maniacs by the dozen. On to Abeardeen!

*****

Maury Meerkat

*****

"The port engine is running a bit hot, Ben. Try shutting down and restarting it."

"Oh, sure, the universal solution. Reboot! OK, down it goes."

Two resplendent white tigers with distinctive black stripes sat in the cockpit of the Aquabear SST. Octavius and Belinda had recently hired the brother and sister away from their jobs hauling freight on 747s for Flying Tigers out of Cincinnati-Northern Kentucky International Airport (CVG.)

Now, at Abeardeen Airport, Benedict and Galatea Tigris were being taken through their paces by Bearyl and Bearnice Blanc. The two polars had been Belinda's flight crew for a number of years and had since gone on to new careers in the theatre and the musical stage. At the moment they were training their replacements. Things were going well, generally. What they didn't know…yet, was they were about to take an unplanned flight into Egypt.

An overhead horn blatted. Incoming message! Bearnice picked up the com device and growled, "Aquabear." It was Octavius. "Hello, Doctor Bear, what's shaking?"

"Is the Aquabear and its new crew fit to travel? We need them to make a fast run to Cairo."

"Well so far, we've only been flying locally but they're doing quite well. If they can jockey around a fully loaded 747 freighter, they should be up to handling this SST. What's in Cairo?"

117

"We believe Imperius Drake is hidden out on a nearby island and up to more of his dastardly deeds."

"Imperius Drake?? We thought he was long dead."

"So did we...several times! He's back, and from a story we haven't got time to discuss, we believe he is going to try to dig up the mummy of a long lost and totally unlamented tyrant, Pharaoh Tsk VI. What happens after that is anybody's guess. We've been in touch with the Egyptian Department of Antiquities and we think they're on board with us attempting to stop him. Our main party will be heading out in the next day or so on the Ursa Major. The Frau and Colonel are on their way down right now to get the plane fitted up once again for desert duty. I'm sending Maury, Otto and Senhor Condor on with them and I'd like you to fly them to Cairo on an advanced recon mission to nose out the Duck's location and circumstances. After you drop them off, return to Abeardeen! Belinda does not want to leave the SST in Cairo and I'm sure you two want to get on with your lives. We'll keep in touch with the advance team from here and then meet up with them when we land in the desert."

"OK, let me talk to the tigers for a minute."

"Hey, you two! Feel up for a quick round trip to Cairo? Bearyl and I will fly with you. *(News to Bearyl!)* We'll be taking three of Octavius' cohorts on a scouting mission to Egypt and leaving them there. A larger group will be going down in the Ursa Major, the C-5A parked over there, after it's fitted out for desert duty. You'll get a chance to meet most of the Great Bear's lineup."

Both cats roared in unison. "Absolutely, when do we leave?"

118

Bearnice returned to Octavius. "They're more than willing."

"Good, the advance team is getting on a Polar Paradise helicopter as we speak. They should arrive there in a couple of hours. How long will it take to have the Aquabear ready to go?"

"About the same amount of time. We'll be ready for them."

She turned back to the felines. "OK, we have some work to do. Ben, let's get this bus fueled up. Gal, plot and file our route to Cairo. Let's try for some over water time, at least on the return trip, so we can go supersonic. That'll be a first for you two. Bearyl, I think we'll need to update the galley and passenger cabin. It's always a wonder to me how that condor can get his wingspan fitted out comfortably in this fuselage. Maury and Otto are the other two passengers. Not exactly giants. I'll check out the cargo bay. I'm sure Condo will be bringing a crate or two of electronic exotica. I assume they'll be setting up their own ground transportation in Cairo. Well, Show Time!!"

# Chapter Eighteen

## *Aboard Polar Paradise Helicopter 1 and Abeardeen Airport*

> *Our advance group is in Abeardeen.*
> *It's a bustling hurry-up scene.*
> *We bid Scotland good-bye.*
> *Two white tigers will fly*
> *On to Cairo where we'll all convene.*

It's difficult to hold a conversation over the "thwup, thwup, thwup" of a chopper's rotors, especially this humongous utility bird, so we settled down to individually collecting our thoughts broken only by an occasional shout. The Colonel and Frau had headsets but we passengers did not. *(Note to Bearoness: The Helicopter com units could use an upgrade.)*

Raamjet, the Uraeus, had given us the name and whereabouts of the fishercat who had transported Imperius and Bigg and then rented them his boat. He lives in a small village south of Cairo, on the Red Sea. Our first stop. The Frau has made arrangements for living quarters in the general area and the Colonel has a desert-capable utility vehicle waiting for us at Cairo Airport. As expected, Condo had stuffed a fair sized crate full of exotic electronics into the copter. A small version of a Ground Penetrating Radar unit mounted on a drone should be waiting for us at Abeardeen Airport. A number of the oil explorers use the equipment. We might need to upgrade it but it's a start.

Otto and I are preparing once more to play detectives. The otter really wants to let loose on Imperius in payback for his crazy and near fatal experiments on him. Condo, who thought he had finished the duck off over the Ohio River is eager for another shot. I just want to see him and Bigg permanently disappear.

It continues to puzzle me that the duck has survived as long as he has. Our team alone has come within inches of killing him off at least twice; thrice, if you count Chita's braining him with a heavy lab vessel. Yet he goes on. I wonder if that serum he takes has a side effect of prolonging life. Oh great, an immortal mad canard!

It's not clear what the situation is with Bigg Baboon. Unlike Imperius, he seems to exist in an unenhanced state. Chita says she saw no evidence of the duck working on him in any way. Baboons are big. *(Hence the name!)* They are quite adaptable. They are also quite intelligent. More so than chimps. But somehow, when the genes for intellectual prowess were being handed out, Bigg seems to have been severely shortchanged. He does have some skills. He's a sharpshooter par excellence with the ray gun. He drives well. Imperius does not. And he's good at all kinds of tasks involving serious lifting. He also made a good living for himself causing strikes and riots in his guise as Commandante Babaloo. He's a dumb heavy for sure but never, never to be taken lightly. *(Sorry about that!)*

The Colonel turned, pointed down and told us to check our seat belts. When you're my size *(and Otto too, for that matter)* it's tough to see out any aircraft windows. But here we were, hovering over Abeardeen Dyce Airport, home to more helicopters than you can imagine. Most of them support the oil rigs. A few, like Belinda's, are private craft used for shuttling the rich and famous.

121

Speaking of private craft, as we touched down, I could finally see the Flying Aquabear, the last functional SST and the pride of the Bearoness' fleet. We skimmed over to the Bearmoral Castle flight facility. *(They'll probably have to change the name to Polar Paradise. Another chore for another day.)* Standing at the foot of the SST's flight stairs was one of the polar twins, Bearnice or Bearyl. Tough to tell which is which unless you're up close. Bearnice wears an anklet bracelet!

As the wolves shut off the engines and the rotors spun down, Otto and I unhooked ourselves, pushed on the door and crawled down the skid support frame. Condo was going to have a little more trouble getting his twelve foot wingspan out and clear. Our one polar welcoming committee bounded away from the SST and picked us up with a heavy duty hug. It was Bearnice.

"Well, you two. Off to mysterious Egypt and the Dismal Duck. I'm not sure I envy you. We're just about ready to move out."

She waved at the Colonel and Frau who were helping Condo lug his equipment crate out of the chopper's cargo bay. Otto and I went back and pulled out our luggage and struggled with transferring the bags to the SST's conveyor belt. Bearyl came trundling down the passenger flight steps, followed by two identical white tigers. The new crew!

"Folks, meet Benedict and Galatea Tigris or the Flying Tigers as we call them. Ben and Gal will be occupying the first seats on the way down to Cairo. Bearnice and I will be going along for the ride and hopefully little else."

Paw shakes all around. Frau Schuylkill said, "We understand you have been flying 747 freighters out of Cincinnati. After you get qualified on the

122

SST, we'd like you to take a shot at piloting Doctor Bear's C5-A, the Ursa Major. That way we can have interchangeable crews for both aircraft. They probably also told you we have an F-15E Strike Eagle, a Twin Otter for minor missions and a fleet of helicopters owned and operated by UUI."

Ben growled and said, "Doctor Bear must indeed be a gazillionaire if he can afford all that flying hardware."

The Colonel agreed. "But you don't know the half of it. Welcome to the fast lane. It'll take a while to get used to Octavius but you two are in for an exciting life. We certainly are. This run to Cairo is just the beginning of a strange situation. I'm sure the polar twins can bring you up to speed on Imperius Drake although I'm not sure even they have heard the latest and greatest. Maury, Otto and Condo can take care of that. By the way, most of the Octavius Bear staff are unique in one way or another. White tiger twins certainly fit that description. Benedict and Galatea. Where did those names come from?"

"Mom wrote classical literature."

Frau Schuylkill laughed, taking the tigers by surprise. "We'll have to set up rooms for you back in Cincinnati and up at Polar Paradise. You'll find Bearoness Belinda is an excellent hostess and an amazing polar sow. Their cubs are astounding. And wait till you get to know Maury, Otto, Howard and Condo. They are a treat. You'll also get to meet the others in our Cat Pack – Chita and Lepi. She's a strange but extremely clever feline. You two will fit right in with her. Lepi's real name is Leperello. He's a Himalayan Snow Leopard and he's Bearnice's singing partner. They're going on tour as soon as

123

you're both checked out on the Flying Aquabear. And Bearyl is going to return to her acting. She's a great Lady MacBearth."

The Colonel interrupted. "You forgot to mention Chief Inspector Wallaroo and Mlle Woof."

"Mlle Woof is the cubs' wonderful governess. She's a Bichon Frisé and as for the bouncing Inspector, I try to forget him as often as I can. He's a genius law officer but he's also hyper-hyperactive. I have to replace furniture every time he shows up, which he already has. He'll wear you out. Anyway, are you all ready to head to Egypt?"

Gal growled, "I think we're all loaded up. One last external check and we'll be good to go."

The Colonel turned to Otto, Condo and me. "Are you guys all set?"

Condo gave a perfect reproduction of Gal's voice and roared. "Where's the Ground Penetrating Radar?"

Gal roared back, "It's in the hold. Want to see it?"

The Condor hopped and flopped his way over to the conveyor belt, folded his wings and rode up into the cargo bay.

The Frau laughed. "See what I mean. We're all a bit strange. How about you two?"

Nods from Otto and me.

Condo stuck his head back out of the loading door and said, "It's all here. I can't test it but it looks like it has gotten plenty of use. If we need parts or repairs, we can probably get them in Cairo or at an architectural dig. Major Akil should be able to help. Let's fly!"

Frau Schuylkill

# Chapter Nineteen

## *A Nondescript Island in the Red Sea*

***Something's different about Bigg Baboon***
***Who for years was Imperius' goon.***
***Now he's come to resent***
***And express his dissent***
***To the Duck and he'll do it quite soon.***

"You, Baboon will have another toy to play with. As soon as Effendi procures the portable ground penetrating radar, you must learn to operate it. I'm sure you will apply the same skill and enthusiasm as you have with the Portable Endoatmospheric Particle Beam Projector."

Bigg nodded his head none too enthusiastically. The Duck noticed but said nothing. He must spend some time reassessing the assignments on this project. Of course, once they have revivified the Pharaoh, there will be a series of major changes. Perhaps none of these three will be required any longer. He must ponder and plan.

"It is almost time we left this depressing island but there are several things that must be done first. Baboon, you will take Effendi back to the mainland and assist him in obtaining the GPR. Then we will be ready to move. I have procured lodging for us near Siwa where we will begin our search for the mastaba of the king. It is no doubt buried under multiple layers of sand. Our GPR will help us find the exact site and the ray gun will do the extraction. You have important tasks ahead of you, Baboon. Hyena, you will remain here with me and begin translating the hieroglyphics I have amassed. When we unearth the Pharaoh's tomb, it is you who must interpret the death scrolls."

Needless to say, the Duck's highhandedness, reflected in his name Imperius, was not sitting well with any of the players. He, of course, was as oblivious of his impact as he had always been. Bigg was beginning to understand why Chita rebelled. He, too, was considering rebelling. Another thing: these two were being paid fabulous sums while he got along on the allowance Imperius gave him. Bigg was jealous and unhappy with this whole operation. He would wait until he had the GPR and ray gun in paw and then go on strike, demanding more money and privilege. If he was a key to this operation, he wanted what he deserved. He and Effendi left for the boat.

Hyena watched them go and then turned to Imperius. "Are you certain you want to bring this monster king back to life? From what little I have read, he was a scourge to all who came in contact with him. How do you intend to revivify him?"

"Ah," quacked Imperius, "my methods are the result of long study and experimentation. I am depending on the skills of the Egyptians who first mummified the Pharaoh. If they followed the standard procedures of the day, I have the ability to reverse them."

"But his brain is probably gone. They would have extracted it along with other internal organs."

"True, but not an issue. I have developed a substitute brain which will suffice for my purposes. I do not need the Pharaoh in his original state. It is his army I want. I need him to transfer their loyalty from him to me. Once he does that, he is expendable. I intend to clone the lions and crocodiles and lead them into battle. There will be an inexhaustible supply of them and they will be able to withstand most modern weaponry. They will also be equipped with copies of our ray gun. It is sufficient for me to be able to strike major fear in our opponents. Surrender is what I want, not annihilation."

Hyena was now convinced that the Duck was well and truly a first-class nut case. However, he was a rich nut case and therefore a potential source of wealth and high living. Hyena had grown tired of paw to mouth existence and wanted to retire in luxury. Perhaps in a Caribbean resort. Anywhere but Egypt. He would play along as would Effendi, he was sure. First they must find the Pharaoh's tomb.

"Where are the scrolls describing King Tsk VI's burial place?"

"Here," said Imperius, handing the Hyena a small electronic tablet. "The original scrolls have all been scanned into the memory of this device. The scrolls themselves are too old and fragile to use directly. They are also too clumsy. You can keep this with you and refer to it as needed. Now, you must begin your search of the hieroglyphs it contains. I want to find that mastaba quickly and your compensation depends on how rapidly you can determine the tomb's location. The GPR will do the rest. Once we have entered the mastaba, we must locate the King's Book of the Dead. Translating that is crucial."

A plan began to form in the Hyena's head. He was almost certain that the Duck intended to kill him and Effendi the moment he felt they were no longer useful. Effendi was probably the first target since his value was principally in supplying logistics. The vulture wouldn't recognize a hieroglyph if he fell over it. Hyena, on the other paw, could string the Duck along by controlling the pace and results of the translations and then leave after killing Imperius off and stealing his money. This nonsense of world conquest could not be allowed to actually happen. An accident inside the tomb was the most likely way of eliminating the Duck.

The Baboon was another matter. He seemed quite loyal to the Duck and was quite strong and no doubt, dangerous. Doing away with him might be a job for Effendi. Right now, the two of them were sailing across the Red Sea on their mission to rent *(or otherwise acquire)* the GPR. Knowing Effendi, he had already captured the Baboon's confidence. He and Effendi must talk when next they meet.

*(Little did he know about Octavius Bear and his teams. Neither did the Duck. Yet.)*

# Chapter Twenty

## *Polar Paradise aka Bearmoral Castle*

*Is the Underworld one universe?*
*Can interment be done in reverse?*
*These are things we don't know.*
*But there's one thing that's so.*
*That damn Duck will make everything worse.*

Bruce, Belinda, Chita and Octavius were awaiting the return of the Colonel and Frau Schuylkill from Dyce Airport.

The Bearoness wondered aloud. "If Imperius wants to keep this crazy program of his a secret, why did he send you a Black Quack, Bruce?"

Octavius, Chita and Bruce answered in a chorus. "His ego! It's what has done him in so many times before."

"Of course, he's not aware of our sessions with the Uraeus so he probably thinks we're completely in the dark about his latest caper." This from Octavius.

"We traced the egg to Egypt. I'm sure he knew we would. Is it possible he's trying to lure us to our destruction?"

"It could be, Bel. He's tried it before."

"You're a scientist, Octavius. Do you really think he can bring that monster back to life?"

"Not in his current condition, Chita, but we may be dealing with a classic case of an alternate universe at work. If the Egyptian Underworld is truly a different world and Tsk VI exists there as a result of the ancient rites of preservation, Imperius may indeed be able to summon him back from his suspended state."

"Whoa there, Ocko!" shouted Bruce. "Do you realize what you just said? You just made a bloomin' case for the dead comin' back to life."

"Only under certain circumstances, Chief Inspector. Only under certain circumstances,"

Wrong response! Chita chirped and slapped her tail on the floor. "What circumstances? Is Howard up on this one? Why haven't we met up with any revivified stiffs, if this so? Honestly, Octavius, sometimes you can be so annoying. Explain yourself, preferably in two syllable words."

The Great Bear huffed and then said, "It would depend on the process that was used to send them to the Underworld in the first place. We don't even know where or what this Underworld is. And yes, I have spoken with Howard and he has some theories but no real proof. We should probably talk some more with Raamjet. Belinda, will you get the cubs. They can establish contact with the Uraeus. We need to know more about Tsk VI and his Book of the Dead."

"Before I get the cubs, you should know they want very badly to come with you to Egypt. So do I."

"Much too dangerous. It's going to be totally unpredictable down there. If he succeeds in his plan no one will be safe."

"You're going to have a small army with you. We can stay out of harm's way. I want to be with you and I don't want to leave the cubs behind. Mlle Woof will be with us, too. She'll keep the two of them in line."

"Let's wait until we hear back from Maury, Otto and Condo. Once we understand the situation, we can make a decision."

"You're not leaving until you hear from them, Right?"

"Right! How about the rest of you? Should I assume you all want to be part of this Egyptian merrymaking?"

Nods all around, including the Frau and Colonel who had just entered the room.

"The Aquabear SST is on its way to Cairo, Herr Bear. You may want to consider adding the Flying Tigers to your expedition. They seem quite formidable."

"Not a bad idea, Frau Ilse *(?!)* How far along are the preparations of the Ursa Major?"

"We are modifying the engine intakes, hydraulics and control surfaces to resist sand and wind. I am less concerned about flying over the desert as landing and standing in the desert. We are replacing the seals on the doors and openings in the fuselage and we have put on special refrigeration units. We are having trouble finding a "cool suit" that will fit you, Herr Bear. We may have to improvise."

*(Readers of the previous Casebooks will know that Octavius and clothing are natural enemies. Not that he lacks modesty. It's just nothing ever fits a nine foot, 1400 pound Kodiak. Tuxedos, especially, are the bane of his existence. A "cool suit" should prove interesting.)*

"Well, see what you can do. It's a shame we're not near UUI. Those guys can invent and fabricate anything. Give Howard a call. Maybe they can make something and fly it direct to Cairo."

*(Money, as usual was no object, especially where beating the Duck was concerned.)*

# Chapter Twenty One

## *Aboard the Flying Aquabear SST*

*On the Aquabear's Egypt bound flight,*
*We've encountered a wonderful sight.*
*Our new pilots are rare.*
*We are flown through the air*
*By two tigers of startling white.*

We made, as they say, a nominal takeoff and we are moving into the upper atmosphere. We can only turn on the supersonic speed over water so we have to content ourselves with loafing along over the European headlands, cities and farmland until we reach the Mediterranean. Even then it may not be worth the extra fuel consumption to push the pedal. Everything seems to be going well with the Flying Tiger flight crew. I want a chance to get acquainted with them and I asked Bearnice to spell them at some point so we can talk. I also want them to get further acquainted with Condo and Otto, two of our "wunderkinds."

Once the SST's autopilot was set to cruise, the two white tigers turned the controls over to Bearyl and Bearnice and emerged from the cockpit. They joined us in the opulent polar bear seats. I had met them when they were first recruited by Belinda and Octavius but I'm not sure they remembered me.

"Hi, I'm Maury Meerkat. We've met but I'm not sure you recall."

Ben chuckled. *(An interesting sound coming from a tiger.)* "How could we forget a short meerkat sidekick surrounded by a nine foot Kodiak and a glamorous member of polar nobility. Glad to see you again, Maury."

Gal waved her pure white paw and purred, "Hello, Maury! Hello, all! What did you want to see us about?"

"Well, first I want to formally introduce you to two of Octavius' associates. This young Otter goes by the name of Otto the Magnificent. He's not the least bit comfortable with that moniker because it was given to him by the maniac Duck we are pursuing. Anyway, it stuck. Besides being part of our crime fighting team, Otto is a first class showbeast and is a client of my theatrical agency. His talents are in the area of teleportation and related skills. When he isn't working with us on a case, he is developing routines with the Bearoness' water show troupe – The Aquabears. That's how this ship got its name. Show biz is in the lady's blood and she continues to combine that with managing the castle, Polar Paradise; working with Octavius; setting up a genetics research center and of course, looking after the cubs."

"We haven't seen the cubs yet, Maury. I hear they are something else."

"They are just about as rare as you are. Maybe more so. Polar-Kodiak hybrids aren't your everyday ursine offspring and they know it. I'm sure they'll be fascinated by you two. That brings up a different subject. We have arranged quarters for each of you at the Shetlands castle and in Cincinnati at the Bear's Lair. I think you'll find both places pretty impressive.

"But where are my manners. One more introduction. This formidable bird is an Andean Condor. Say 'hello' to Senhor L. Condor, lately from Brazil.

He is one of the world's greatest experts on telecommunications and computing. He continues to perform wonders just about every day. We call him Condo."

Both cats said, "Hello Condo!" and were shocked to hear him reply in an exact reproduction of their voices.

"Pardon me," said the bird. "My own little personal joke. Condors do not have a natural voice box so most of my species are mute. Dr. Bear and his engineers have helped me develop an artificial vocal device that translates my thoughts directly into appropriate sounds. We put some extras in the box like the ability to speak in over a hundred languages; the ability to mimic other voices; *(That came in handy during several of our adventures.)* and we have miniaturized it to fit under the skin or at least under my feathers. All in all, a handy piece of equipment."

Otto spoke up. "Hi! Glad to meet you! Benedict and Galatea! Interesting names but then again my real name is Hairy Otter. The Otto thing just stuck. Are you called the Flying Tigers for real?"

Ben replied, "It's actually the name of the air freight company we flew for but since we were the only tigers working for them, we got the name as well. They occasionally trotted us out at sales conventions or expos. It got to be a bit much. But tell us about this maniac Duck we're taking you to meet."

I responded. "Imperius Drake is a Class A villain. He is clearly insane, part of which has been brought about by a serum that transforms him from a mild mannered Mandarin Duck into an evil genius. He lost his one true love as a result of his experiments. She died trying to stop his crazy work. He has a special hatred for the genetics profession that shunned and ridiculed his efforts. He attempted to assassinate a thousand of them at a convention in Las Vegas. We stopped him but just bearly.

He also detests Octavius, Belinda and Chief Inspector Bruce Wallaroo. You have to meet Bruce. He's a real piece of work from Australia. Brilliant but rambunctious! There is also a major war between the Duck and Chita. You'll definitely have to meet her. She was part of his Black Quack gang but deserted him. He, in turn, tried to kill her and they have been making attempts on each other's life ever since."

The tigers were just beginning to get a taste of the extraordinary group they had signed up with. They were usually the ones who were considered exceptional. In this crowd exceptional seemed to be routine.

I continued. "Now, you guys signed up to fly airplanes and we don't expect you to get tangled up in our crime fighting but we do need to keep you aware of what we are doing. The three of us are an advance party tasked with finding Imperius and if possible, cutting him off at the pass."

Gal asked, "How do you know what he's up to? He doesn't advertise, does he?"

"In a way, he does. His ego is cosmic. He sent one of his egg-shaped Black Quack weapons to Bruce, knowing full well we'd track it back to his location – Egypt. But this all got started as a result of an appearance on, believe it or not, the game consoles of the twin cubs by a Uraeus, a demigoddess cobra charged with guarding tombs. She had become aware through her network of ancient deities and sub-deities of Imperius' little caper.

138

She convinced Octavius that Imperius was set on bringing King Tsk VI back from the Underworld. The Pharaoh is a pretty nasty individual and while we're not exactly sure what the Duck has in mind, it can't be for the benefit of civilization. The Pharaoh's tomb has been lost up till now. Raamjet, the Uraeus, can't give us its physical location. She's in a halfway spot between two worlds. Oh yes, I'll also have to clue you in later on some of the work we're doing on identifying alternate universes."

At this point, the tigers were torn. On the one hand, all this was more than a little flustering for a pair of jet jockeys. They'd had some interesting moments working for Flying Tigers but nothing to match this situation. Should they hand in their resignations when they got back to the Shetlands? Or-or-or was this right up their feline alley? They needed to parley.

Ben growled and said, "I think we better be getting back to the controls. After all, this a training flight for us. But we'll want to hear more about your mission and about the rest of the Great Bear's crew. Sure different from hauling freight."

We shook paws all around and they went back to the cockpit.

Condo looked over at me and said, "Do you think we spooked them?"

Otto said, "I wouldn't be surprised."

I would have shrugged my shoulders if I had any.

# Chapter Twenty Two

## *At Polar Paradise*

*We have Raamjet once more on the line.*
*She reveals that she's semi-divine.*
*She describes how the King*
*Did not feel Ammit's sting*
*But he's caught by Anubis' design.*

The two cubs rocketed into the playroom with Mlle Woof bringing up the rear. "Are we going to Egypt, Poppa? Are we?"

"We haven't decided yet. I have to talk with Raamjet right away. Do you think you can reach her?"

"Did Uncle Condo fix it up so we can reach her from anywhere?"

"He did, but she needs to know how to reach us. Right now, I want you to use the play station and call her."

With an explosion of pushing and shoving, Arabella got to her console first and started loading up the Egyptian Tomb game. McTavish ran over to his keyboard and started up his copy. There would be wall-to-wall Raamjet.

After the opening "splash" screens flashed on, ominous Egyptian background music and a menu of options followed. Keys clicked, mice flew around the pads and there they were in the depths of an ancient tomb.

McTavish shouted at the console microphone. "Uraeus! Raamjet! It's us! Bella and Tavi! Poppa needs to talk to you right now. Come out, come out wherever you are!"

In the distant murk, shining red lights slowly emerged. The glow of the snake's eyes increased in intensity and suddenly a reptilian face filled the screen. "Ah, my young ursine friends. Welcome! And welcome to you, Seeker of Justice. I see your noble spouse is with you as well as the members of your court. Greetings to all! What is the urgent matter we must discuss? Has the despicable Duck begun his infamous expedition?"

"Not yet but we believe it will be very soon." Said the Bear "We have sent three of our most capable agents to Cairo where they will launch a search for him. We believe he has his headquarters on a small island in the Red Sea. We need to get more clarification from you about how King Tsk made his journey to the Underworld."

The Uraeus replied. "The Duat or what you call the Underworld is the realm of the dead. The Book of the Dead is a guide to the deceased to enable them to make their passage safely. There are many dangers on the route and not all spirits survive. They suffer a second death. The Ka or spirit of King Tsk VI did not complete the journey. It lies in a suspended state, neither destroyed nor elevated. He has escaped for the moment the vengeance of Ammit, the Devourer but his heart has been found out of balance by the goddess Maat, embodiment of justice and truth. Anubis has chosen to isolate his spirit rather than destroy it."

"In the case of the Pharaoh, his Book of the Dead is a "coffin text" inscribed on the surfaces of his sarcophagus. Therein lies my burden. I must protect the mummy's case from being accessed and defiled. In the wrong claws, it may be possible to summon the King's spirit back from the halfway state in which he rests. I believe this is what the diabolical Duck intends to do. Exactly why, I do not know."

"You should also know that when he died, a number of his followers died with him. They too, rest unjudged. They are known as the Languishing Leonine Legions and the Pharaoh's Phalanx. A small army of lions who cruelly conquered all who defied the King and a unit of crocodiles, sworn to protect him with their lives. When the Pharaoh's barge sank, they were with him and perished in the Nile. It is strange that the crocodiles did not survive. It is believed that the barge was sunk by members of the King's court who managed to kill the Phalanx before they could save King Tsk. Most other members of his retinue survived the disaster. Remarkable, is it not?"

"So, Raamjet, do you believe that one in possession of the King's Book of the Dead could summon his spirit back to this world."

"It would take great skill and understanding and of course, they would have to deal with me first. I am a formidable being."

Belinda asked, "Are you immortal?"

"I cannot die naturally but I believe I could be killed. It would be a fierce fight for someone to overcome me. Of course, the first thing he must do is find me. But if he actually enters the crypt, then I must challenge him."

142

"We intend to keep the Duck from doing that but I must warn you. He has in his possession a highly destructive weapon which he has not hesitated to employ in the past. Fortunately, we have several too. It is our intent to prevent him from using the device. Right now, our advance team is trying to track him down as well as locate the Pharaoh's tomb. When we hear from them, we will bring the main body of our group down to Egypt and to the mastaba. Meanwhile, our communications specialist, Senhor L. Condor has created a linkage system so we can converse with you regardless of where we are. You need only continue to summon us as you have done so far. Our system will do a relay."

"Are the Egyptian authorities aware of all this?"

"Yes, and we are cooperating with them fully. They have limited resources and are reluctant to engage themselves unless and until the Duck shows himself and his intentions. We have dealt with him in the past and believed him dead several times. He has eluded his demise thus far. We wish to change that."

"The gods of Egypt will help and inspire you. I must speak further with Anubis, perhaps even Osiris. Farewell for the moment."

Octavius switched off the displays and turned to the assembled team. "Why does he want to bring a tyrant's spirit back from the dead?"

Chita spoke up. "Given his ego, I can't imagine Imperius bowing down to some despot. I think he wants those ghostly lions and crocodiles. Remember he's a crackpot geneticist. He may believe he can clone an army of fierce immortals and use them to move on to world or maybe, cosmic conquest."

143

"You may well be right, Chita. You may well be right."

# Chapter Twenty Three

## *On the Red Sea*

*So Effendi astutely explains*
*Why the shrewd Duck has taken such pains*
*To keep out of sight*
*Til the timing is right*
*In the search for the Pharaoh's remains.*

After a few near capsizes with Bigg Baboon at the helm, Effendi took over steering the fishercat's boat. The sea was relatively calm but the wind was gusting, often changing direction in the process. They reefed the sails and proceeded on power with the old engine wheezing and occasionally backfiring. To call the boat an old tub was to pay it an undue compliment.

"I don't understand why we have this crummy old wreck," said the Baboon. "The Emperor has lots of money. We could have rented a modern fishing boat."

"Aha, my friend, you miss the point. Once again, Imperius Drake has demonstrated his cleverness. Who would suspect a disreputable craft like this being used by the world's most resourceful criminal? Certainly not the Egyptian Police. They would be looking, if they are looking at all, for a speedy yacht able to outrun a government patrol. No, your employer is indeed crafty. Besides, we will not need this boat for much longer. One more round trip to pick up Hyena and Sahib Drake and we will be through with it."

"Good, I don't like that stinking island. The sooner we're away from it, the better. I like the savannas and the desert."

"Well, you will have a great opportunity to renew old acquaintances with the sand. How did you come to be the Duck's associate if you lived in a savanna?"

"I was forced into it. I don't know why he was there but he threatened Chita and me with one of those crazy eggs he has...the Black Quack! We ended up working for him. Chita ran away after he tried to murder her because she betrayed him. That was years ago. She's been trying to kill him ever since."

"This Ms. Chita sounds interesting. Perhaps I shall meet her one day."

"You might, if she finds out he's here. How did you end up dealing with the Emperor?"

"A long story. Suffice it to say he has had needs in the past for someone to facilitate his activities in Africa. That's what I do. I facilitate. Strange that you and I have never met before! Although in my business, I try to keep an extremely low profile. Ah, we are about to reach the dock. Please get ready to tie us up. One of my associates should be here with the Ground Penetrating Radar as well as suitable transportation for the desert. Once we have haggled for the equipment, we can go back and pick up Sahib Drake and Hyena."

"Oh, swell! Two more boat rides."

146

"We must also cross the Nile to get to the oasis at Siwa. There is a bridge at Luxor. I do not believe it is advisable to go to Cairo or Giza and the ferries can be watched by the police. The bridge will be safer."

"Where is Siwa and why do we want go there?"

"It is far to the west. Sahib Drake believes that the mastaba of the Pharaoh is located there. I do not know why he thinks that. He will not share his information. But he has picked a very long route from the island to the oasis."

"What's a mastaba?"

"A tomb. This one is probably buried deep under the sand, if it is there at all. This could turn out to be a wild duck chase. *(Chuckle!)* But he pays well!

"He pays *you* well!"

"Ah," thought Effendi, "Do we have some dissatisfaction in the ranks? A mistake on the Duck's part, especially if this baboon is going to be handling weapons and equipment. I shall have to keep a watchful eye."

As they got off the boat, a nasty looking camel approached.

"Ahlan, Ali! It is good to see you again."

"And you, Effendi. Who is your friend?"

"This is an associate of my nameless client. His name is Bigg Baboon."

The camel stared at the baboon. "The name is appropriate. I have the equipment you ordered. I do not like to linger here so let us get the business over with quickly. I have procured a four seat desert ready utility vehicle with an equipment trailer. The Ground Penetrating Radar is in the trailer but it can be handled by someone with moderate strength. There is a cart and spare batteries as well as a ruggedized PC. The PC has an extensive user's manual. Who will be using the device?"

"I will," said Bigg. "I also manage the ray gun."

"What ray gun?" This from the camel.

Effendi slid in before Bigg could answer. "It is a device to speed up excavation. It can remove sand and stone at an amazing rate. And before you ask, it is our client's closely guarded secret and not available for reproduction or sale."

He looked at Bigg and shook his head. For once, the Baboon got the hint and shut up.

Effendi said, "We will leave the vehicle and trailer here where you have stored it but we will take the GPR back with us. Now, let us discuss payment.

Haggling and negotiation! Effendi tried to keep Bigg out of the discussion so he could go back to Imperius and hike up the prices he had paid the camel. Bigg didn't seem to care about the give and take and wandered over to the trailer and pulled out the GPR unit mounted on a small cart. Looking around for a ramp or gangplank he could use to haul the unit aboard the boat, he let go of the cart's handlebar. It started rolling toward the dock as Bigg stood there transfixed. The camel ran over and blocked the wayward trolley's movement. He stared at Bigg and then Effendi. "This is the guy who operates a ray gun?"

The vulture shrugged.

After jostling the cart aboard the fishing boat, taking care of last minute transactions and saying goodbye to the camel, they headed the dowdy dhow back toward the island.

"Bigg, do you think you can handle this radar unit?"

"Oh sure, I'm a whiz at computers and techie stuff."

Effendi wasn't too confident. But perhaps this baboon will be the downfall of the Duck's crazy plan. Somebody needed to stop him. *(But only after Effendi and Hyena were handsomely paid!)*

# Chapter Twenty Four

## *Cairo International Airport*

*See the locals all quizzically stare*
*At the team from the sleek Aquabear.*
*We're a very odd crew*
*And the plane is strange, too.*
*Did a circus just drop from the air?*

I'm not sure who or what got the most attention as we disembarked from the Flying Aquabear. The SST itself? The matching polar bear twins, Bearnice and Bearyl? Condo with his twelve-foot wingspan? The two white tigers, Ben and Gal? Otto and me? *(Probably not! Nobody ever notices a meerkat.)*

Nevertheless, we encountered a number of curious stares, especially when Major Akil came to meet us. Greetings all around! He arrived in our utility vehicle driven by a Pharaoh Hound named Hamid. Hamid was assigned to us by the Egyptian Antiquities Authority for several reasons. One: He knows Egyptian roads and terrain like the back of his paw. Two: He is well trained in arms and defensive activities. Three: He is highly knowledgeable about ancient Egyptian history, customs and antiquities. And Four: None of us can drive. Otto and I are too small and Condo's wingspan makes it impossible for him to deal with conventional vehicles.

Major Akil had also brought a customs inspector with him. The inspector gave our luggage a cursory nod and asked to see what was in the crates. The major explained the need for the GPR drone unit and assured him that all this was with the strong approval of the Egyptian Antiquities Authority. SST refueled, passports stamped, vehicle loaded, pawshakes with the major and off we went. First stop, Marsa Alam on the Red Sea and the fishercat the Uraeus told us about.

As we were rolling out of the airport gates, the Aquabear started taxiing toward the runways. The Flying Tigers had taken over the flight deck while the polar twins sat by. They would reach Scotland before we reached our destination. Bearnice and Bearyl, two of my talent agency clients, were ready to go back to the stage and leave the flying to the Tigris twins. I suppose the Frau and Colonel would also check Ben and Gal out on the Ursa Major, Octavius' aerial warehouse and stealth weapons platform. That aircraft was a major contributor to foiling Imperius Drake's thousand-fold assassination attempt at a Las Vegas genetics convention. We'll see what adventures it will be involved in this time around. We'll also see how the tigers take to the Great Bear's crime fighting activities. They thought they would only be doing supersonic shuttle duty for the Bearoness. Surprise!

*****

Much as I enjoyed being back in desert climes, boredom settled in pretty early. Actually, we were rolling through a landscape irrigated by the Nile floods. Not this time of year, thank goodness. When we left, Hamid had projected an arrival at Marsa Alam in about 8 hours. We'd been on the road for six and dusk was beginning to set in. We would be arriving at night.

Condo had established contact with Raamjet who told us the fishercat's name was Farouk and he was well known on the waterfront. Actually Marsa Alam is a resort of moderate size. I don't think we will have any time for relaxation or cavorting.

I asked Hamid what he knew about King Tsk VI. He confirmed the stories we had heard, adding that many historians doubted the Pharaoh ever existed. On the other paw, I really doubted that Imperius Drake would be mounting a major campaign to track down a phantom pharaoh. The duck may be nuts but he is also quite well informed.

"We believe the king's mastaba is somewhere near Siwa."

"Then why are we driving south to a Red Sea resort when we should be heading west?"

"Because we going to try to intercept the Duck before he sets out. I don't know why he chose an island in the Red Sea to establish his headquarters but that's what he did. We wouldn't even know that if Farouk, the fishercat hadn't told Raamjet, the Uraeus, where he was."

"The Uraeus is real?"

"Oh, very much so, my friend, and it seems, so are the Egyptian gods. The Underworld is authentic. We have been making a study of alternate universes for quite a while. They do exist. And the Egyptian Underworld seems to be a prime example. You may want to rethink some of your assumptions about what is myth and what is reality. In a few days you'll meet the rest of our team. It's led by Dr. Octavius Bear, a famous scientist and

152

detective. He is convinced that parallel universes not only exist but from time to time interact with our world. I know that sounds fantastic and it took us quite a while to come to that realization. But we have several of the finest technical minds in the world accumulating, sifting, analyzing and evaluating a vast array of inputs. At this stage, we believe the evidence of the reality of alternate worlds is damn near incontrovertible. Now, you may think we are all a bunch of kooks dealing with bizarre criminals but I think you'll find that Major Akil also buys into our theories. And he is quite a skeptic."

"Well, this is certainly more than I bargained for. And all I thought I'd be doing is playing mechanical camel driver and possibly warding off an insane duck."

"That insane duck is a dangerous individual. We've had several near misses with him including an attempted mass assassination. It's easy to underestimate him or write him off as a fruit loop. He's none of the kind."

"Hmmm!"

"That's what they all say!"

The time and the roads wore down and we finally entered Marsa Alam just as the last shards of sunlight were glistening on the Red Sea. We headed down to the fishing docks hoping that Farouk might still be around. A local tavern keeper pointed him out to us. He was sitting curled up on the forecastle of a pretty down and out motorized fishing dhow. Strange that he should be on the boat. We thought he had rented it to Imperius.

I went over and introduced myself and told him we had come at the direction of the Uraeus to find him. We needed to know where the Duck and his cohorts were.

Farouk let out a plaintive cry and said. "They're gone."

"Gone?? Where? How?"

"They brought the boat back this afternoon, loaded up a big truck and trailer and headed out. I think they were going west. There were four of them. The duck and his baboon, a hyena and a vulture. They paid me well for the use of the boat. I am sorry. I promised the Uraeus I would be vigilant but I had no way of following them."

"If they wanted to go west with a large desert truck, how would they go? How would they cross the Nile?"

Hamid said, "They wouldn't use the ferries. They might use the Luxor Bridge to the south. I doubt they'd want to go through a city."

Farouk howled and said, "I heard the baboon say something about Luxor and Armant."

I turned to Otto and Condo and said, "Well, they're obviously out ahead of us. I think we need to get on the horn with Octavius. As he often says, "The game is apaw."

# Chapter Twenty Five

## Red Sea and Polar Paradise

*Score one point for the Duck's gamesmanship.*
*It appears we've been given the slip.*
*Seems he's now heading west.*
*So I strongly suggest*
*We get on with the rest of our trip.*

Octavius had just awakened from one of his narcoleptic episodes. His arousal was assisted by the loud and insistent ringtones of his smartphone. *(in his case an extremely smart phone!)*

"Bear here!"

It was me, Maury, on the other end. "We just arrived at Marsa Alam and it seems our Anitidae foe has flown the coop, literally. He's on his way west in a large utility vehicle with Bigg and two other animals I can't identify – a vulture and a hyena."

The Bear looked around, spotted Chita and asked. "Do you know anything about a vulture or hyena who would be tied in with Imperius?"

"The vulture might be a bird named Effendi. Imperius used him from time to time in Africa. Another one of his facilitators. The hyena is news to me. But in Egypt, a hyena would not be an unusual henchbeast."

155

"Where are the Colonel and Frau?"

Belinda replied, "They're back from Cairo. They're still at Abeardeen Dyce Airport."

"Tell them to stay there. We are going to have to move out earlier than I intended. Make sure they have the ray gun. *(He actually used that term.)* We have another one here to take with us. Ask them to dragoon a couple of mechanics to disassemble and load a couple of scout helicopters on the C-5A. We're going to have to mount an aerial search for the mastaba around Siwa as well as catch up with Imperius. I suppose Senhor Condor has the GPR drone with him. Are those Flying Tigers ready, willing and able to join us?"

"I don't know but I'll call the Frau. I don't think we should involve Bearyl or Bearnice, although they'll be torn between their careers and knocking over Imperius. Now, Octavius, let's get something else settled. I and the twins are going with you. If she wants to come, Mlle Woof can join us."

Ever the practical strategist and now doting husband and father, Octavius knew when he was defeated. "All right, but they will have to be kept out of danger and trouble. No point in telling you to stay protected. Who else is up for this venture?"

In rapid fire order, Chita, Bruce and Mlle Woof agreed. Chita and Bruce wanted to get their paws on Imperius and the Bichon didn't want to let the cubs out of her sight, especially if their mother was going to be joining in the fight.

"OK," roared the Bear. "Let's get moving. I want to be at the Abeardeen airport in the next couple of hours. Pass that on to the Colonel and the Frau and check on those tigers. But first get the cubs in here. I need to talk to Raamjet"

Mlle Woof scurried off to retrieve Arabella and McTavish who came bouncing into the room shouting, "Can we go? Can we go?"

Belinda grabbed them and said, "Yes. Poppa says you can go but you're going to be under strict rule, do you understand? Mlle Woof and I will be watching you all the time. This is not a game! This is very serious and dangerous. I hope I don't live to regret it. Meantime Poppa wants you to call Raamjet. He needs to talk to her."

"The cubs ran to the console, logged on and started calling the Uraeus. "Raamjet, it's us. Arabella and McTavish. Poppa needs to talk to you right away."

Once again, the gleaming red eyes appeared on the screen as the cobra came closer. "I am here, young ones. Where is the Seeker of Justice? And I greet you, Spouse of the Bear!"

"I return your greeting, O Uraeus. Octavius will be with us momentarily. We have news and it is not good."

The snake hissed and said, "I have already spoken with the fishercat. He tells me that the much despised Drake is underway toward Siwa. As you say, this is not good news. However, it will not be easy for him to find the tomb. Even I do not know its exact location. I live with the Pharaoh's sarcophagus in its Underworld form but I do not know where it is in terms of your universe. The coffin is a nexus point where the two worlds connect. I am on one side. Whoever reaches the tomb will be on the other."

The Great Bear replied, "You are confirming much of what we believe about alternate universes. There are, no doubt, many places where our world and others intersect. Locating and identifying them is a major research project in which we have taken a substantial lead. However, that can wait until we deal with the threat at hand. I have a team on the ground pursuing Imperius Drake as we speak. Since they are using the same type of vehicle that the Duck is employing, I'm not sure whether and how they will catch up with them. That is why we are getting ready to fly our massive aircraft to the desert area near Siwa. Among other things, it will be carrying two search helicopters and a device known as Ground Penetrating Radar. This will help us to identify the most likely location of the King's mastaba. Unfortunately, we believe Imperius Drake is similarly equipped. He also has a major advantage at the moment. We believe he has with him an animal skilled in reading hieroglyphs and other symbologies. He will be searching for the King's Book of the Dead. Do you know where it is?"

Raamjet hissed once again. "The Book of the Dead is the coffin itself. It is covered inside and out with prayers, instructions and recordings. As I told you, King Tsk is in a halfway state, neither at peace in the Underworld nor restored in your own world. Can this infernal duck actually bring the Pharaoh back to life?"

"We don't know. He has done some extremely unlikely experiments in the past, most of which were complete failures. Are you familiar with the term 'Clone'?"

"A technique for producing genetically identical beings based on an original. I am informed of such things. Do you believe that is the Duck's intent?"

"He is an expert geneticist. He may not intend to activate the original as much as produce a modified clone. What good that would do him is unclear."

The cobra's eye gleamed. "It may not be the King himself that he wishes to reproduce. In that same halfway state are the warriors and personal guard of the Pharaoh's who perished with him in the Nile. The Languishing Leonine Legions and the Pharaoh's Phalanx. Fierce and rampaging lions and a unit of barbaric, huge crocodiles, all slavishly devoted to the King. It may be these whom he wishes to revivify and multiply."

"With the Duck's technology, they could be made into a catastrophic threat. He has been on a mission of world domination for many years. This would be the most fantastic effort yet. As I have said, he seldom succeeds. We must make sure he doesn't this time."

"We will be leaving Scotland shortly. The cubs and the Bearoness will be with us as well as Colonel Where, Frau Schuylkill, Inspector Wallaroo, Chita and the cubs' governess, Mlle Woof. I believe you met them all on one of our last calls. We also have a pair of white tigers who will pilot our aircraft. It will take us about eight hours to reach our destination at Siwa Oasis Airport.

From there, we will launch our search helicopters and radar to help locate the mastaba, if indeed that is where it is. I believe the Duck and our advance team will also be in the vicinity. Just one other incidental question. I assume you are immortal!"

"In a manner of speaking, yes! Although I exist at the pleasure of Osiris. At some point, I expect to be relieved of this guardian burden but not yet...not yet. Why do you ask?"

"In case Imperius meets you and tries to destroy you."

"He will find that difficult, indeed."

"Good, we will keep contact with you and you know how to reach us. Goodbye for the moment."

"Farewell and keep your children safe and secure. I greatly enjoy them."

Octavius called for Dougal, the hotel manager and dog-in-charge. "How many helicopters do we have on the property right now?"

"One large utility craft and one medium transport, sir"

"OK, we'll need them both to get us all down to Abeardeen. The Bearoness and Inspector Wallaroo will do the flying."

"All right, everyone! Let's get moving!"

*****

An hour later, two helicopters with Aquabear livery took off from the Castle helipad. In the large craft, piloted by Belinda sat Octavius, the twins, Mlle Woof and Chita surrounded by crates full of equipment, clothes and a massive amount of snacks prepared by the Palace chief cook, Mrs. McRadish. Bruce Wallaroo piloted the other chopper filled with additional supplies, two models of the ray gun and a large supply of conventional armament. Given his unique and near suicidal techniques in flying helicopters *(see Book One: The Open and Shut Case)* no one was particularly eager to join him as he bounced around the sky. He had a perfect accident-free record but many stomachs gave out lengthy and pitiful distress signals while he was pilot-in-charge.

Octavius had called ahead to Abeardeen to check on the progress of loading the C-5A. They were on schedule. The Flying Tigers had agreed to join the expedition. It turns out that they are helicopter certified. Another big plus. On the way to Siwa Oasis, they would take turns with the Frau and Colonel at the controls and acting as navigator and flight engineer.

Next call – Maury in the Egyptian desert. But first…

# Chapter Twenty Six

## *Somewhere in the Sahara*

*I can hardly describe life as grand*
*As we slog our way through desert sand*
*On a treacherous route*
*In a rapid pursuit*
*Of the Duck and his desperate band.*

Bigg Baboon, in the driver's seat of the utility vehicle, chose to ignore the rants of the Duck as they bounced along a sand covered road heading west toward Siwa Oasis. Effendi was in the shotgun seat, occasionally offering directions. In the back with the Duck, Hyena was attempting to pass on the known history and lore of Pharaoh Tsk VI. In each instance, Imperius knew better, contradicting the wayward Egyptologist at every turn.

"What I want from you, Hyena, are not history lessons but flawless translations of the hieroglyphs and symbols we encounter in the King's Book of the Dead. I have placed my trust in you. A thing, as Effendi knows, I seldom do! It will not go well if you fail me. Baboon, have you and Effendi completely tested the Radar? It too must not fail."

Effendi answered, "The GPR performed flawlessly during all of our rigid tests. *(Under his breath: "as we both told you at least a thousand times.")* It will not fail."

"What about the ray guns?"

Bigg muttered. "They're fine!"

And then, a sound none of them had ever expected to hear. The Duck shouted, "Are we there yet?"

## Farther East in the Sahara

As Hamid contended with the barely existent roadways, I got on the phone with the Colonel and Frau, still in Abeardeen. "Hi! Can we exchange progress reports? We're crossing the Sahara in not-so-hot pursuit of Imperius and his three thugs. We still believe he's heading for Siwa Oasis. It's about a sixteen hour drive. We've been on the road for about six hours now. There are only a few places to stop but refueling is turning out to be a non-issue so far. We have a major supply of gas and water in auxiliary tanks. I don't know about Imperius. I doubt Bigg would think that far ahead but the other guys with him are desert rats and should know what they are doing. Who knows? We may run into them yet, if they have had any problems. I don't know what they are going to do once they reach Siwa. What's your status?"

The Colonel replied, "We are just waiting for Octavius and his entourage to arrive by chopper. They should be here shortly. We are going to have a small army on board: Octavius; the Bearoness; the two cubs; their governess, Mlle Woof; Chita, and Inspector Wallaroo. We will also have two flight crews: Ilse and I plus the two Flying Tigers. We have two scout helicopters in the hold and a utility vehicle that hopefully, is suitable for desert travel. You guys have the GPR drone, I trust. We have two copies of the ray gun as well as several refrigeration units. I don't know how those ursines are going to stand up to the Saharan heat."

163

"It gets quite cool at night. Yes, we do have the GPR but I doubt we'll get to use it before you arrive. What's your estimated flying time?"

"About eight hours to Siwa Airport. We can use their runway but it will be a near thing. I've checked it out.  Major Akil got all the permits and paper work taken care of. He'll probably meet us at Siwa."

"You may beat us there. This road trip is a doozey. It's a shame we couldn't cut him off back at the Red Sea. Did you say the cubs are coming along? Is that safe?"

"No, but they can twist their parents around their little claws. I hope their governess can keep them in tow."

"Condo has checked the GPR out and it seems to be working well. Otto is also boning up on its use so we can have multiple teams. Once you arrive, how long will it take to get the helicopters airworthy?"

"I forgot to mention, we are bringing two mechanics and a load of spare parts along to service the choppers. Condo will service the drones. Desert sand and whirling rotors are a lousy combination. The mechanics aren't too happy but promises of bonus payments from the Bearoness smoothed things out. With luck, we can get the ships airborne in about six or seven hours after we arrive. Does the Duck have any airpower at his disposal?"

"We don't know but I don't see how he can operate without a whirlybird. Of course, he's a whirly bird, himself. Have you ever thought of just how much time and effort we have all devoted to dealing with this nut case?"

164

"Too damn much, Maury! I hope we can put an end to this jerk this time. Although, he has survived several times after we thought he was dead. Anyway, here comes the first of the Castle choppers. We'll call when we are leaving. Say 'hello' to Otto and Condo!"

After I hung up, that nagging question climbed back into my meerkat brain. Do we have any idea where the hell we are going? Suppose the crazy Duck is wrong. Suppose all our suppositions are cockeyed. Suppose there is no tomb and no Tsk VI in this universe. Who knows where the Uraeus actually is. She didn't seem to know, either. I'm sorry Howard isn't with us. Our porcupine expert on alternate worlds is back in Cincinnati. There's an idea. I'll call Howard.

# Chapter Twenty Seven

## *Abeardeen Dyce Airport*

*You may think that Belinda is wrong*
*But the cubs are both coming along.*
*Will that spirited pair*
*Misbehave in the air?*
*We'll find out if they will before long.*

As they bounced out of the helicopter, the cubs stopped short and gaped at the huge C-5A. "Momma, is that the airplane we're going in? It's gigantic! Is that Poppa's plane? Your Aquabear would fit inside it."

Belinda chuckled, "All the planes and helicopters belong to both Poppa and me. And yes, we're going to Egypt in the Ursa Major. Do you know what Ursa Major means?"

Arabella piped up, "Big Bear, just like Poppa." They both fell into a fit of laughter and swatting each other.

Belinda grabbed them and said, "You two promised to behave. I hope this isn't your idea of behaving. Now, come on! We have things to do. Mlle Woof will help you get on the plane when the time comes. Meanwhile, you stay with her and don't get in the way. As you can see, they are loading two helicopters onto the ramp. The mechanics removed the rotors and they're going to tie the ships down inside. Colonel Where and Frau Schuylkill are in charge of the flight."

As she was talking, the Flying Tigers sidled up. Galatea growled a muted greeting and said, "Good afternoon, Bearoness! Nice to see you again. Thanks once again for hiring us on. Although we didn't expect to be off on a wild duck chase in Egypt."

Belinda frowned. "Is that a problem, Gal? Are you and Ben reluctant to be part of the expedition? It may turn out to be dangerous."

Ben's turn. "Not in the least, Bearoness. It's just that you folks seem to be full of surprises. Actually, it adds interest to the job. Sure beats hauling a load of freight all over the sky. And these must be your young offspring. Hi! I'm Benedict *(call me Ben)* and this is my sister Galatea."

"Call me Gal. Like you, we're twins."

McTavish stared at them. "But you're white. Aren't tigers supposed to be orange?"

"Most are. but we're the cats of a different color. You guys don't look like Polar Bears or Kodiaks. You're different, too."

This set the cubs off on another round of laughter.

At this point, Mlle Woof introduced herself to the tigers and herded the cubs off to a hangar until it was time for boarding. Chita and Bruce Wallaroo came over to shake paws and to load up their personal belongings.

Gal looked over at Ben and said, "It looks like the Flying Tigers are going to be part of a Flying Circus." They both grinned and watched as Octavius did his check list number with the Colonel and Frau. In the middle of the process, Octavius suddenly yawned and slipped down into a fetal position. Sound asleep courtesy of narcolepsy. The tigers stared open-mouthed. "Is he OK?"

Belinda chuckled, "Something else you need to know about the Great Bear. He suffers from occasional narcoleptic episodes. It's the result of work that he performed on himself to prevent the need for hibernation. He'll be out of it in a few minutes. It can be a problem, however. That's one reason he never drives, flies or uses dangerous equipment. He has also been known to keel over in the middle of some crucial activity. We've learned to deal with it and anticipate it. Maury, Octavius' sidekick, is a past master at contending with his problem."

The tigers stared at each other and then at Octavius who was blissfully snoring. "Well," said Ben, "we need to start buttoning up the Ursa Major."

Gal shrugged and said, "Curiouser and Curiouser!"

Within the hour, Octavius was back on his feet, roaring orders at all and sundry and generally being the pain in the tail he can so skillfully be. Everyone and everything was secured in the "belly of the beast" and the Ursa Major came to life. Frau Ilse and the Colonel were at the controls while the Flying Tigers took up station as flight engineer and navigator. The ursine cubs were disappointed that the C-5A had no fuselage windows. On the other hand, Mlle Woof, who was not a particularly serene flyer was delighted by the lack

168

of the passing skyscape. She set about giving the cubs more lessons in Egyptian history, especially what little was reliably known about Pharaoh Tsk VI.

"He sounds like a pretty bad guy," said McTavish.

"I'm sure he was," the dog replied.

"So, why are we interested in him?"

"Because another bad guy, Imperius Drake, is interested." This from Belinda. "And we want to stop whatever terrible thing he has in mind."

"Who is Imperius Drake, Momma?"

Before Belinda had a chance to answer, Chita chirped and said, "He's a mad scientist, kids. He's brilliant but he always seems to come up with crazy ideas that blow up in his evil face. I should know. I was with him for a while but now I want to see the world rid of him. In fact, I think we all do."

"Uncle Bruce, do you know Imperius Drake?"

"Oh, you bet your booties, I do. I've been chasing after him for a long, long time. I thought he was dead any number of times but the dippy duck keeps coming back along with that baboon of his, Bigg Baboon."

"What's a baboon?"

"A large kind of ape. Bigg is dumb as they come but strong as a...as an ape."

169

And so it went. Octavius snoring in his especially re-designed cargo container. Snacks and conversation. The cubs buried in their electronic tablets. The mechanics continued to work on the choppers, installing sand filters and special lubricants. On the flight deck, the tigers checked in several times with Maury and the ground team who were wending their rock strewn way toward Siwa. It looked like the plane would get there first. Major Akil was also on his way from Cairo in an Egyptian military helicopter. Rendezvous: Late evening Cairo time zone.

# Chapter Twenty Eight

## *The Western Sahara*

*Howard Watt thinks the Underworld's real*
*As the ancient inscriptions reveal.*
*Is it in the Duck's head*
*To restore the long-dead?*
*That idea doesn't have much appeal.*

"Howard? Maury here! We're out in the desert and I'm not too sure how well our communications will hold up. I need some expert opinions and input from you on the possibilities of the ancient Egyptians connecting with an alternate cosmos that they called the Underworld. Is it a real place or just support for wishful thinking?"

Howard Watt, porcupine, techie genius extraordinaire and Octavius' mastermind on all parallel universes! "Hey Maury! Finally back in a desert. Hot enough for you?"

"Yeah, it's not the Kalahari, my old digging grounds, but its close enough. I've been freezing my tail off ever since I came to work for Octavius. This change is great. But I may be the only one who thinks so. So what's your verdict?"

"From all that I've seen and heard, the probabilities are extremely high that some type of alternate world exists that accommodates the spirits of the dead. Any number of religions base their entire ethic on the existence of a next life which may be glorious or devastating to the deceased. They also propose the idea of a halfway state, a sort of limbo or purgatory, so the idea of the Pharaoh being stuck in transit is not so unusual."

"What about this idea of a Book of the Dead, Howard? A sort of instruction guide to achieve immortal bliss."

"Also not unusual. The concept of minor gods or angels acting as directors and protectors during the journey seems to be common. This Uraeus, Raamjet, whom you are dealing with clearly exists and she cites a number of other so-called gods as being involved in the transition process. I'm inclined to believe it."

"OK, Howard, now the $64,000,000 question. We think our cracked-brain nemesis, Imperius Drake, is going to try to revivify the king as well as his soldiers and bodyguards. What's your take on that?"

"I can well imagine him trying. I wouldn't take bets on his succeeding. The mummification process seems to be one way to me but I'm no expert. If he's going to attempt to establish contact with the king, that's a real long shot. On the other hand, what about this Uraeus? Is she alive in the physical sense or a spirit? She seems to straddle both states. And her longevity as an active sentient being is phenomenal."

"We know the Duck has experimented with clones. One theory Marlin and I have been kicking around is that he will create physical copies and attempt to infuse a spirit of the dead into them. He'll bypass the actual mummy or in the case of the army and bodyguards, their corpses and go straight for reanimating the ghosts."

172

"As we both know, Maury, Imperius is capable of trying anything and he's just brilliant and resourceful enough to make some progress. If your theories are correct, this is the wildest thing he's come up with yet. But what purpose does all this serve other than to glorify the Duck's already enormous ego."

"Again, we may be way out in left field but there is one thought that he wants to create a fearsome and potentially immortal army to achieve world conquest. As long as he controls the spirits of the lions and crocodiles that serve the King, he can manufacture and re-manufacture a limitless supply of disposable troops using those animating forces over and over."

"What about the King, himself? He's not going to sit idly by."

"That's something we haven't figured out yet unless Imperius is just going to use him as an initial link to the troops and then destroy him physically and spiritually once he has gained control."

"And he's going to pull all this off with a baboon, vulture and hyena?"

"Plus several ray guns and Ground Penetrating Radar. The real question is where the hell is the King's Book of the Dead? Could papyrus survive unprotected for this long?"

"It may not be papyrus, Maury. In the case of royalty and aristocracy, the Book of the Dead was often inscribed on the walls, floor and cap of the sarcophagus. The mummy's case!"

"Oh boy! That puts a different spin on things. No wonder the Uraeus is so protective of the coffin. We're getting close to Siwa Airport. I can see the Ursa Major parked on a sideline. I want to replay our discussion with Octavius and the team and get you tied into the planning. Meanwhile, I would love to know where our friend, the Duck is. Or maybe I don't. Talk soon, Howard!

I turned to Otto and Condo and said, "Howard thinks the Book of the Dead is inscribed on the coffin itself. I'll have to check that with Octavius. We can see what the Uraeus has to say about it. Otto, I hope you've been working on your 'now you see me, now you don't' skills. I think we're going to need them for following Imperius and his thugs around."

"That would be ironic. Maury. After all, he's the one who created the elusive Otto in the first place with his injections."

"Everything about that nutty Duck is ironic. This time I hope we see the last of him and that stupid Baboon. I'd love to know a bit more about the Vulture and the Hyena. The fishercat Farouk said the Vulture was making all the arrangements. I'll bet the Hyena is a hieroglyphics expert. Maybe Major Akil can shed some light on that."

"Anyway, there's the Ursa Major taking up more than its share in airport space. We're still a couple of miles away but that bird is in a class of its own when it comes to hugeness."

Condo got on the radio and signaled where we were. The Colonel responded and told us to come right up to the C-5A. Octavius wanted to hold a conference ASAP. Oh boy! Here we go!

# Chapter Twenty Nine

## *Elsewhere in the Western Sahara*

*As the Siwa Oasis comes near*
*The conspirators' fears are severe.*
*Now which way should they go?*
*Does Imperius know?*
*Thoughts of ditching the Duck reappear.*

Bigg steered around rocks and ruts, occasionally getting stuck in the sand. Of course, Imperius would not lower himself to help push the vehicle out. He sat in the back seat bemoaning the inefficiencies of Egyptian roadwork, Bigg's driving and the world's lack of appreciation for his infinite genius.

The thought occurred to Effendi that he should cut his losses and wring the Duck's neck. Only that infernal Black Quack device held him back. Hyena seemed of the same mind. They weren't quite sure where Bigg was on the subject but clearly his blind obedience to Imperius was beginning to show holes.

So it went, until they came to the border of Siwa Oasis. Imperius had rented a substantial house in the outskirts from which they could mount their expedition. Effendi checked out a map with several of the locals after they had wandered off course a couple of times under the Duck's faultless guidance.

"We shall take up residence here. From the information I have gleaned, we are not far from the area in which the King's mastaba is buried."

Hyena raised a vestigial eyebrow and asked. "How do you know that, Imperius? There have been a number of searches over time for the tomb. All ended in failure. What do you know that they didn't?"

"That, my friend, is my secret. Suffice it to say that with my direction and the fine tuning of the GPR, we will come upon the tomb in short order. Baboon, get the radar ready! Tomorrow morning, we will rise with the dawn and seek out the Pharaoh's resting place."

Hyena retorted, "The Pharaoh's mummified remains may be there but it will not be his spirit's resting place. He is in the Underworld, if he is anywhere."

"And that, Hyena, is why you are with me on this pursuit. We need the Book of the Dead and an accurate interpretation of its directions to seek out and bring back his shade. Failure is not an option!"

Murmuring under his breath, Hyena started to unload the scrolls and other support documents he had accumulated in the last few days. He would need them to interpret whatever instructions were left behind in the Book of the Dead. First, they'd have to find the book, assuming of course, that they find the tomb. This Duck has taken arrogance and self confidence well beyond world class heights. 'Failure is not an option.' Indeed! If things go well, it will be because of the Duck's unfailing wisdom and perception. If, on the other hand, they do not, as is most likely, he, Effendi and the Baboon will be to blame.

While Hyena's principal motivation is out and out greed, there is also an outlandish fascination attached to this comedy. Finding and resurrecting a long lost Pharaoh who from all the tales told about him, deserved to be trapped in the darkest depths of Underworld forever! Cloning his armies to achieve world conquest! He's a nut! But he's a very rich nut. Hyena's goal must be to exit this farce with the largest possible payout, escaping with his life and limbs in the process. Oh well, nothing ventured...

Similar thoughts were racing through Effendi's mind as he helped Bigg carry the equipment and supplies into the house. He had assisted Imperius before and had become not accustomed to, but at least familiar with his eccentricities. But now, the Duck had retrogressed far beyond being eccentric. He was absolutely, certifiably mad. The thought occurred to the Vulture of taking off in the middle of the night, leaving them stranded. Unfair to Hyena but no doubt, he could take care of himself. Effendi's part of this exercise was almost over anyway. He had "facilitated" the project. They could find substitute transport at the oasis. He would be leaving behind a chance for increased riches but he would be getting out with his skin intact. He had no doubt that the Duck intended to kill them both once he had reached his goal. He would certainly do them in if they did not succeed. Nothing for it! Flight, at the earliest opportunity.

Bigg had different thoughts. He had come to increasingly resent his treatment by Imperius. He had faithfully, even slavishly, obeyed the Duck throughout the years and had gotten damn little for his efforts. Now, if this screwball project succeeds and Imperius has the Pharaoh under his control along with his armies, he would have little need for Bigg. Bigg didn't want to escape the way Chita did. Bigg wanted revenge. Bigg wanted control. Bigg

177

wanted to be Imperius Bigg. The Vulture and the Hyena could be problems. He'd have to deal with them. They must not succeed. The King must not be brought back. Bigg would make sure of that. The time had to be right. He would wait, but not for long.

Imperius had withdrawn into the house, leaving his "minions" to see to the administrivia and preparations. Tomorrow at dawn, the great journey of discovery would enter its final phase. Supremely confident in his personal genius *(in spite of an almost unbroken track record of failures)* he would begin his ascent to world conquest. Nothing and no one would stop him. Even that accursed Bear.

On reflection, perhaps he had been too hasty in revealing his presence by sending the Black Quack to that stupid Wallaroo. No doubt, they know he is in Egypt. They probably traced the egg that far. Beyond that, he was sure they know nothing. *(Ironically, he knew nothing of the Uraeus and the Egyptian gods who had invoked the aid of Octavius and his team.)* But how sweet it would be to bring his long standing nemesis to his furry knees. Probably too much to ask for the moment. If the Bear is in Egypt at all, he is probably wandering hopelessly around the arid sands of the Sahara. After establishing his cosmic realm he would have ample time to deal with Octavius Bear. Ample time!

# Chapter Thirty

## *Siwa Oasis Airport*

*The Great Bear holds a Council of War*
*And he gives out assignments galore.*
*The Uraeus has read*
*The King's Book of the Dead*
*And informs us just what it is for.*

"OK! Time is of the essence. We need to find that tomb before that crazy Duck does!"

This from Octavius, who had called an "all hands" meeting inside the C-5A. Present: The Great Bear, Chita, Inspector Wallaroo, the Frau and Colonel, Condo, Otto, the Bearoness, Hamid, Major Akil, the Flying Tigers, the two aircraft mechanics and oh yes, me. Mlle Woof had the two cubs out walking *(jumping, cavorting)* around the area.

Major Akil spoke up. "I wish I shared your confidence that the mastaba exists and is in this vicinity. There have, as you know, been several expeditions that couldn't uncover anything. This could turn out to be a wild duck chase."

"True, Major, true! Actually, I'm less interested in succeeding than I am ensuring the Duck fails. He is the threat and we know he is here, probably somewhere in or near the oasis. And that leads me to Item One: I want to launch the spy drones to search him out. There are still a few hours before

179

darkness and we can start our scans immediately, then switch to night vision. I doubt he would set up inside the oasis proper. He's probably out on the perimeter. I also doubt we'll find him, personally. He's not likely to be moving around outside but we may get lucky and track down the Baboon or his Vulture and Hyena associates. Frau Ilse and Colonel, can you set that in motion? I also want you to check out the Ground Penetrating Radar and the ray guns."

Nods from the wolves as they moved out with one of the mechanics.

"Item Two: I want the Ursa Major sealed from the weather and the sand. Shroud the engines. Cover up the landing gear. Close up the hatches. Ben and Gal! Will you and the mechanics see to that? Let's also get the helicopters desert ready. I want a rotating presence inside this aircraft at all times. There is plenty of fuel for the portable generators and we can keep the air conditioners on when we need them. It will get pretty cold after dark. Our quarters are right near the airport's freight terminal and we can move in there shortly."

"Item Three: Condo and Otto! Let's get our communications systems fully operational ASAP. Also, I want to talk with Raamjet as soon as we close this session. Bel, I want you to join me for that. She seems to have great rapport with you."

"Item Four: Maury, you've had a long conversation with Howard about the Underworld and its parallel universe characteristics. Let's discuss that in just a moment."

"Inspector and Chita, I want you to put your heads together and try to strategize how the Duck is going to behave. I know that's tough but you two know him as well, if not better, than any of us. If he does succeed in finding the tomb and the Pharaoh, how will he go about the resurrection process? What about the Vulture, Hyena and Bigg?"

"Major, obviously you and Hamid can call your own shots. I value your presence and input but we are here as your guests. Let me know how and if you want to proceed."

"Octavius, I need to brief my superiors. Don't worry! I will be quite selective in what I tell them and I also need to speak with the Siwa Oasis authorities. They will be told that a survey team is here to explore archeological possibilities under the aegis of the Antiquities Commission. It won't be the first time. But this aircraft, your equipment and your team will certainly be a novelty. I will discourage any interference on their part. They will not be told anything about Imperius Drake. But I am sticking my neck out. If he succeeds or causes any damage or disaster, I will probably end up behind bars or in front of a firing squad. It is crucial that you cut him off before he gets that far."

"I understand fully, Major. That is exactly what we have in mind. Actually, I want to kill him off. He has survived too often in the past and it is clear that I am his Number One adversary with the rest of my team and family as close seconds. Incarceration won't work with him. He has proven to be much too dangerous to continue with his plots and plans. I honestly believe he has world or cosmic conquest in mind this time. We cannot let him escape.

However, we will also have to deal with his associates. I hope you are prepared to arrest them under the authority of the Antiquities Commission."

"Yes. It would give me great pleasure to run Effendi and Hyena in. I don't know Bigg but I'll be happy to arrest him as well."

"You may not get the chance. The Baboon has always been right at the side of Imperius. We'll probably have to deal with them as a pair. Now, Maury, clue us in on your conversation with Howard."

I reviewed the conversation we had about the Underworld being one or more parallel universes and said I thought it would help if Howard and the Uraeus communicated. Then I brought up the idea that the Book of the Dead was not a book in the usual sense. Howard seemed to think it was highly likely that the Book was actually inscribed on the surfaces of the Pharaoh's coffin and catafalque. There was no assurance, of course, that Imperius thought this was so. In fact, he might even damage the mummy's case in an effort to gain control of the King's languishing spirit. We agreed that our next stop needed to be a multi-path conversation with the Uraeus.

Meanwhile, two drones, equipped with thermal imaging for night time surveillance, were being launched and sent off on a perimeter sweep of the oasis. The Colonel and the Frau were controlling their progress and recording anything that might be suggestive of the Duck's presence and activities. We are all but positive that he is here. We need to find out where and rapidly.

Condo was putting the finishing touches on the communications links. Belinda turned to Octavius and said, "Let's allow the cubs to establish first contact. They adore Raamjet and she is fond of them. Condo can bring

182

Howard into the picture and you, Maury and I can question her further about the Book of the Dead."

"I'm not sure I want the cubs involved any further in this, Bel"

"Octavius, we need to keep them occupied and feeling important. Mlle Woof is doing a wonderful job of reining them in but they need to see and be with their parents, too. Once we allowed them to come, we left ourselves open to having to deal with them. I know, I know. It was my idea. But I am their mother."

This struck Octavius as a non sequitur but he decided not to point it out. "OK. Fetch them in here. When we get finished talking to Raamjet we can all go over to our quarters and wait on developments."

Suddenly, a 'thud' and Octavius rolled over with a mighty snore. Narcolepsy had scored again. Assuming he'd be out of it shortly, Belinda squeezed out of the forward access door and went off in search of the cubs and Mlle Woof. Condo and Otto were running test messages and conversations over the com links. I looked over at Chita and Bruce who were busily comparing notes and history, shaking their heads and making notes in their UUI notepads.

I assumed Ben and Gal were sealing and hardening the Ursa Major against possible damage. They were also getting the search helicopters ready for desert deployment. At first sign of any Black Quack activity picked up by the drones, the choppers needed to be ready to go. The Frau and Colonel would turn the drones over to the Flying Tigers and they'd head out in the well armed helicopters with Otto, Condo, Bruce, and me on board. The Major and

Hamid were getting into their vehicle to head into the oasis and meet, greet and make nice-nice with the local authorities.

The C5-A's access door flew open and two brown and white missiles scrambled through and tumbled onto the floor of the cargo hold. "Poppa, Momma says we can talk to Raamjet. Can we, Poppa? Can we?"

The twins stared down at Octavius who was still out for the count. "What's the matter with Poppa, Momma? Is he all right?"

"Poppa's just taking a short nap. He's very tired. He'll wake up in just a minute."

Groans and snorts from the Great Bear. Opening one eye, he was greeted with a pair of pointed black noses front and center in his face. They backed away as he struggled upright. Without missing a beat, he said, "Hello, little ones. Ready to talk to Raamjet? Uncle Condo has it all set up. Momma's going to help and so am I. Let Mlle Woof get you settled."

Screens flickered. Background noises rang across the cargo bay. "Raamjet, Raamjet! It's us! Arabella and McTavish! Come and meet us! Come and meet us!"

Darkness suddenly broken by two piercing red lights. The Uraeus was approaching. A resounding hiss and her face filled the screens.

"I greet you, young ursines. You are here in Egypt. In Siwa? Was that wise, mother of this precious pair? There is danger here."

Octavius interrupted. "They are being well protected, Raamjet, but we appreciate your concern. They are like their parents. Eager to see goodness triumph. We could not leave them behind."

The snake gave what seemed like a shrug. "I must not presume. I greet you all, especially you, noble lady. What news and what plans are in progress?"

Belinda nodded in acknowledgement and said. "We must confer with you in depth, oh demi-goddess. We are sure the demonic Duck is here in the Siwa area. We believe the King's mastaba is somewhere nearby. We know you cannot give us a physical location but we must also know the nature of the tomb and especially the coffin. Does it, as we believe, contain the Pharaoh's Book of the Dead?"

"It *is* the Pharaoh's Book of the Dead. The prayers, formulae, directions, curses, warnings and procedures are all inscribed on the surfaces of the coffin and the pier that supports it."

"Then, the Duck must actually reach the coffin if he is to attempt to raise the King? He cannot call on him from afar."

"That is true. Even then, it will be difficult, if not impossible for him to carry out the reversal process without stumbling or making a fatal error. I will also ensure that he cannot succeed. Although I live in two worlds at once, I can face him down in your universe."

"Will that make you vulnerable to an attack?'

"Probably, but I am much closer to being immortal than he is."

Octavius growled and said, "We are expending much time, effort and resources to ensure he does not get that far. We have our entire team, highly efficient technology and massive energy to prevent him from finding, entering and defiling the tomb. He plans to, in a sense, revive the King and call forth his soldiers of lions and crocodiles. We believe he will attempt to clone a huge army of them and lead them in world conquest. He is mad."

"No more mad than the Pharaoh," said the Uraeus. "I have the magic of the gods to assist me. What does he have?"

"Formidable weapons! Some of which he stole from us. He is capable of piercing the walls of the mastaba or opening the mummy's case with equal ease. Needless to say, he can also murder and maim. You must not underestimate him. It is easy to assume he is simply a deranged nuisance. He is much more than that. Otherwise, we would not have come here in such force and with an array of our own weapons. I have been battling him for years. We thought we had disposed of him several times. In each instance, he survived."

"By all means, call upon your gods and their magic but do not become overconfident. If we can, we will stop him before he even reaches the tomb but we are prepared to pursue him into the depths. Now can you describe for us how the tomb is arranged and the nature of the coffin and its supports?"

"Your offspring should be able to tell you how the tunnels and rooms of the mastaba are arranged. They traveled through them several times while playing their game."

Arabella squealed. "You mean it's real. We were following real paths?"

"Yes, young one. You never reached the mortuary hall where the coffin rests but if you remember, you did pass through chambers that contained the royal artifacts. You stole a few."

Arabella blushed, "Oh Raamjet, I am so sorry. We thought we were just playing a game. The one who captured the most treasure was the winner. I never took any of it away with me. Neither did McTavish."

"You couldn't. I was there to prevent any actual theft. Nonetheless, if you start up your game again, you will see how the paths, rooms and tunnels are arranged. I will then show you the way into the royal chamber where the Pharaoh's mummy rests."

"Seeker of Justice! The King's Book of the Dead is inscribed on his catafalque, case and coffin. The hieroglyphs must be spoken with great accuracy and in proper order for them to have any effect. You say that the evil Duck has an expert with him who is learned in sacred writings and formulas. Who is he?"

Octavius, who with the rest of us was listening to all of this in startled wonder, came to himself and replied, "We think his name is Hyena or so Farouk, the fishercat told us. He is, in fact, a hyena. Major Akil of the Antiquities Commission knows of him. He has from time to time worked for the Commission but has recently let himself out to the highest bidder in any form of antiquities theft or related crimes. We have reason to believe he is quite skilled in interpreting the ancient writings."

187

"He is unknown to me but if what you say is true, we must seek him out and prevent him from reaching the Pharaoh's Book of the Dead. Without him the Duck will be helpless."

Octavius replied, "Not helpless, just delayed. He has enough resources to seek out another translator if he needs to, but I agree. Hyena must be stopped. We have plans to capture him and turn him over to Major Akil. But first we must find all four of them. We have devices called drones that fly by remote control and are capable of tracking down targets in great detail. We will have them in the air shortly."

"Meanwhile, what can you tell us of the Pharaoh's Phalanx and the Languishing Leonine Legions? Where are they? How many of them exist? How can Imperius Drake bring them back? I assume they are not included in the King's Book of the Dead."

"You are correct, Seeker of Justice. There are over two hundred lions and fifty crocodiles. They were hastily buried and cursed by the priests to remain imprisoned in a halfway state of existence. I do not know why they were not simply sent to the dark regions. They are not with the King but it is highly possible that he can summon them. That is one and maybe the only reason Imperius Drake wants to resurrect the Pharaoh. To bring back his minions and build an army of ferocious ghosts. How the Duck plans to do that and then control them is a great question. I believe he will have to keep the King under his thrall to manage the lions and crocodiles. Perhaps he intends to serve as the Pharaoh's Grand Vizier. No easy task."

"Perhaps, but the Duck, no doubt, thinks he is capable of mastering them all. His ego is boundless. He is clearly insane. He has a history of spectacular failures but that has not stopped him from creating even more outlandish plots. Even when they collapse, his fiascos often do major damage. We cannot even allow him to begin this one."

# Chapter Thirty One

## *A House Outside Siwa Oasis*

*The Hyena tells all that is known*
*About soldiers the Duck wants to clone.*
*Both the lions and the crocs*
*Are a terrible pox.*
*The Baboon thinks he's spotted a drone.*

The setting sun cast a crimson aura on the Great Sand Sea that surrounds Siwa. Old ruins, mud brick hamlets and rustic homes sharing space with palm trees and olive groves sank into the advancing shadows. Here and there, pale electric lights flickered on as the Siwans prepared for another evening's routine.

In one house, events were anything but routine. Imperius Drake was holding court. "Hyena, I wish to be told all you know about the Pharaoh's Phalanx and the Languishing Leonine Legions. Where are they? How many of them exist? I assume they are not included in the King's Book of the Dead." *(Narrator's Note: Does any of this sound recently familiar?)*

Hyena chuckled to himself. "Now he wants to hear from me. He didn't hire me for ancient history lessons, he said. What an egotistical jerk! Oh well, it's his money."

Aloud: "The scrolls do not clearly reveal the fate of these formidable animals. It is believed that they are somewhere separate from the King. The

190

lions numbered in the hundreds. The crocodiles were fewer but no less dangerous. None seemed to have survived the sinking of the Royal Barge. This may have been deliberate. Their bodies were cursed by the priests and interred without mummification. I do not believe you will find any reference to them in the Pharaoh's Book of the Dead. You will, no doubt, have to bring the King back and then convince him to call for his minions, assuming he will know where they are and how to restore them. This is clearly what you westerners call a 'long shot.'"

"I shall have the King in my claws. We must be able to threaten him with being returned to his eternal captivity or worse. Only I will hold the key to his continued earthly existence. He must obey my will or he must suffer the consequences. I will not be thwarted by a second rate Egyptian monarch."

Tired of the Duck's incessant rants, Bigg shambled outside and looked around. Plans were forming in his little-used mind. Plans to replace the Duck as Imperius Bigg. With the exception of the buzz and chirps of insects and lizards, near silence enveloped the area. He could still hear the Duck carrying on with his bombastic quacks. But suddenly, he heard something else. A whirring in the air off to the side of the building. His acute ears perked up as he listened to this different, steady buzz. No insect he knew could make that sort of noise. It wasn't an airplane – too soft. What else? What else could produce that drone? Drone! A drone! Somewhere up there! He couldn't see it. Too dark! And it wasn't flashing any lights!  But he could track the sound. Was it just a stray toy or were they being watched?  Should he tell Imperius? The Duck would probably scoff at him as he usually did.

He went back inside and gestured to Effendi who was also bored out of his mind from the tirades of the Duck. The vulture hopped over to him and Bigg put his fingers to his mouth to tell him to stay quiet. He signaled for him to follow him out the door. The sound was still there. Bigg looked at the bird, shrugged his shoulders and pointed into the sky. He mouthed the word "drone." Effendi spread his wings and hopped into the air in the direction of the whirring. As he neared it, the sound intensified and then rapidly disappeared. The bird circled and then returned.

"What do you think, Vulture? Are we being watched? By who? *(Bigg's grammar left a bit to be desired.)* Should we tell Imperius?

Wheels turned in Effendi's head. If they were indeed being watched, probably by the Egyptian Antiquities Commission, he would have to put his escape plan in action later that night. He knew nothing of Octavius and his crew. Nor did he know the sizeable amount of technology that the Bear was capable of using. He could deal with the authorities, if necessary. He might even risk turning Imperius in.

"No, Baboon. He would just ridicule us as being spooked by the desert and this crazy project. Let's wait and see if it returns. It might be perfectly innocent. Unfortunately, I didn't get a chance to identify it. It's pretty small."

They walked back into the house. The Duck didn't notice. He was too intent on cross examining Hyena and boasting of his own prowess. Effendi suggested that they all get to bed early if they were to rise at dawn. Miracle of miracles, the Duck agreed.

The Vulture crept into his own room and began to gather his belongings and money he had carefully swiped from the Duck's bulging billfolds. He would have to wait until the others were asleep. And then…

# Chapter Thirty Two

## Siwa Oasis Airport

*Our lunatic villain, the Duck*
*Has encountered a bit of bad luck.*
*He expected next day*
*To be well under way.*
*But Effendi has stolen the truck.*

Back at the C-5A the Colonel was piloting two thermal imaging drones at once while The Frau and Condo checked out the Ground Penetrating Radar. Suddenly a flare appeared on the screen of Drone #2. The wolf looked carefully at the image. He had been picking up stray individuals all evening. This was right above a modern house with a large utility vehicle and trailer in the courtyard. Two figures were standing and looking in the direction of the drone. Suddenly, one of them, a large bird, took flight and headed in the direction of the Unmanned Aerial Vehicle (UAV.) The other figure, still on the ground looked familiar. A large ape or a baboon. Bigg Baboon? Is the bird Effendi? The colonel pulled the drone away and circled far enough out to muffle the sound of the UAV's motors. The bird landed again and the two figures shambled and hopped back into the house. After waiting a few moments, the colonel closed in on the structure and vehicle. No one else came out. The few lights in the house blinked out.

"I think we have a live one," the wolf shouted. Octavius, Frau Ilse, Condo and I all converged on the UAV console. "It's a house on the Siwa

194

perimeter. Big enough to accommodate four or more animals plus a fair amount of equipment. There's a large utility truck and trailer outside. I'm not absolutely certain but there were two characters standing outside listening to the sound of the drone. One sure looked like Bigg Baboon and the other was a large bird, possibly a vulture. That might be Effendi. The bird flew up searching for the UAV and I pulled it away in time. I don't think he actually saw it. Anyway, at the moment, I'm hovering just out of their hearing range and I'll make another pass in a few minutes. I'll keep Drone #1 scanning elsewhere just in case."

About 3AM, the drone detected movement in the courtyard. One figure. Looked like the vulture. He was trying to unhitch the trailer from the truck. The Frau who had taken over for the Colonel, called for Octavius.

"Herr Bear, I think one of our conspirators is going to do a cut and run. The Vulture whom we believe is Effendi has just detached the utility vehicle from the trailer. I suspect the trailer holds weapons and probably one or more Ground Penetrating Radars. Only a guess on my part. Unfortunately, we are not set up for audio. He must be making some noise but so far no one else has emerged from the building. OK, now he is in the truck and moving away at a high rate of speed. Should I follow or remain watching the house?"

"Bring the other drone over to the house and stay on the truck with this one. Is the Colonel awake?"

"I'm here, Octavius," said the wolf, stifling a yawn.

"Is one of the helicopters ready to fly? I'd like to capture the occupant of that truck."

"I'm on it. Ilse, patch the drone's video through to me in the chopper. The vulture's not flying. I suspect he's using the truck because he has taken a few valuables with him but the trailer would have slowed him down too much. A shame! That means Imperius, if it is Imperius, still has all of their weapons and equipment. Where's Condo? If he decides to ditch the truck and fly away, we can still grab him. A condor can outfly a vulture any day. We'll see what his priorities are."

Condo was already squeezing his 12 foot wingspan into the helicopter's bubble as the Colonel leaped into the pilot's seat. The chopper rose and headed off across the oasis. Drone #2 was keeping pace with the truck as it headed onto a perimeter road. Clearly, the Vulture was doing a bunk.

It only took a few minutes for the helicopter to catch up with him. The Colonel turned on his own thermal imaging system and began tracking without the drone's input. He got out ahead of the vehicle and then flew directly back into its path, shining the copter's spotlight straight into the cab. The truck swerved, left the road and tumbled into a steep ditch, rolling over on its side. The condor half jumped, half flew out of the bubble and landed atop the wreck. The vulture was inside and not moving. The Colonel brought the chopper down and joined the condor in dragging the vulture out of the cabin. Then he reached in again and pulled out a large briefcase the bird had with him."

"Let's get out of here. This thing could be on fire in another minute."

They tossed the unconscious vulture and the bag none too gently into the rear seat of the chopper with Condo holding him down. The Colonel took off and made a beeline for the airport and the Ursa Major. Octavius, Inspector Wallaroo, Otto and I were all waiting as the helicopter settled in and the rotors spun down. We pulled the now semi-conscious vulture out of the cabin and pushed him into the hold of the C-5A.

Octavius stared down at the bird. When he thought he was fully awake, the Bear said, "Ustaaz Effendi, I presume! I am Octavius Bear. Welcome to my world."

The vulture looked up at the towering mass of brown fur and then at the others surrounding him. "Who are you? Why am I here? Why was I attacked? Where am I? What do you want with me? I am just a humble merchant. You have made a very serious mistake."

"I think not! You may be a humble merchant but you are deeply involved with that mad duck genius, Imperius Drake. That bag you were carrying has enough evidence to lock you up."

"I don't know any Imperius Drake."

"Oh, yes you do. You also know Big Baboon and a hieroglyphics expert named Hyena. We will get a final identification shortly from Major Akil of the Egyptian Antiquities Commission. We are aware of your proposed efforts to find and resuscitate the Pharaoh Tsk VI as well as his guards and army. I don't think the commission will take kindly to your plans."

"How do you know all this? Who has betrayed us?"

"Ah, so you do admit that you are part of the crazy Duck's scheme."

"I do nothing of the kind. I told you. I don't know any Emperor Drake."

"Imperius Drake. And nobody has betrayed you. Our information comes from an unusual but highly reliable source. A source I doubt you'll want to meet."

He was interrupted by Otto who had been monitoring the communications channels. "Octavius, we have a problem and it won't wait."

"Tie the vulture up and leave a call for Major Akil to meet us here. Tell him we have one of the Duck's co-conspirators as our guest. What is it, Otto?"

"The airport tower is sending out warnings. A major sandstorm is rising on the Great Sand Sea and it's heading in this direction."

"All right, everybody up. Get Belinda, the cubs and Mlle Woof out of the house and into the Ursa Major. If we have to, we'll ride it out in the plane. It's heavy enough to stand off most major storms. Colonel, Frau! Call back the drones and let's get the helicopter back inside the ship. Then let's move it to the other end of the runway where there's less chance of flying debris. I don't want to unseal the engines. See if we can borrow a tug from the airport. Do we have enough food and water on board?"

Chita, who till now had been a silent observer, volunteered to check and restock the ship's supplies. "Octavius, I've met this Vulture. He's done

198

some work for Imperius in the past while I was still with the Duck. He calls himself a facilitator."

"Well, let's see him facilitate this one. Otto, how much time do we have before the storm hits?"

"Less than three hours!"

"OK folks, let's move."

# Chapter Thirty Three

## *A House Outside Siwa Oasis*

*A startling conclusion is made*
*By the Duck. He has just been betrayed.*
*Yes, Effendi is gone*
*How the Duck carries on!*
*He dissolves in a manic tirade.*

5 AM.  Bigg was rummaging in the food locker and decided to go out to the trailer to get more supplies. Something seemed different. He scratched his head and then noticed that the trailer was attached to nothing. Where's the truck?

He bounded back in the house shouting, "It's gone! It's gone!"

Oddly enough, Imperius was up and about. "What is gone, Baboon?"

"The truck! The truck!"

"What do you mean – gone? Where did it go? Who took it?"

"It's not there. I don't know!"

At that moment Hyena wandered in.

"Hyena, did you move the truck? Where did you put it?

"I haven't been near it since we got here. Where is it?"

"We don't know," cried the Duck. "Effendi! Effendi! Go wake him up, Baboon!"

Bigg ran off and came back just as quickly. "He's not in his room. Maybe he took it. Maybe he went for more supplies."

Hyena laughed. "In the middle of the night? You can't be serious. I'm willing to bet our hook-beaked associate is driving like crazy to put as much distance as he can between him and us."

Bigg scratched his head again. "Why didn't he just fly away?"

Imperius shouted, "Because he wanted to deprive us of transportation, that's why. He may have ditched the truck somewhere once he got a safe distance away and then flew away. Go look for it, Bigg. I doubt you'll find Effendi but bring back that truck!"

Once again the great avian strategist was airily giving orders and leaving their execution to his subordinate. How Bigg was going to search for a truck without transport of his own didn't seem to occur to Imperius. It did occur to Bigg.

"What do I use for wheels?"

"I don't know. Borrow a camel! Use your resourcefulness."

Once he got the words out of his mouth, even the Duck realized that resourcefulness was not Bigg's strong suit. "Hyena, go with him. Find that vehicle."

Suddenly, it dawned on Imperius that another reason the bird stole the truck was that he was carrying things with him. Things he couldn't carry while flying. Effendi was gone and he had taken his traveling bag with him. Documents, valuables, cash and several artifacts that Imperius had acquired were all missing. So were a couple of pistols.

The Duck flew into a rage. "Betrayal! Betrayal! When you find him, Baboon, kill him on sight."

Hyena intervened. "Wouldn't it be wiser to bring him back and question him? What did he have in mind? Was he going to the authorities? If Octavius Bear is in Egypt, perhaps Effendi was going in search of him."

"Yes, find Effendi and bring the traitor back.

# Chapter Thirty Four

## *On Board the Ursa Major*

*As he tries hard to brazen things out*
*The caught vulture is stuck, without doubt.*
*Facing Major Akil*
*He denies he would steal.*
*But the police know what he was about.*

At that moment, Effendi was tied up and lying against one of the cargo pods inside the cavernous fuselage of the C-5A, watching the proceedings as the Bear's team prepared to ride out the impending sand storm. He had no idea of what had become of his bag. He was sure the wolf or the condor had taken it while he was unconscious but now it was nowhere to be seen. He looked up as a Mau Cat in military garb strode over to him.

"Good evening, Effendi. A rather awkward way to renew acquaintances but there you are and here I am."

"Hello, Major. I am the victim of mistaken identity. These American ruffians wrecked my vehicle, assaulted me and took my belongings. I must protest to you as an official of the government."

"Good try, Vulture, but your protest is falling on deaf ears. I am aware that you have been aiding and abetting Imperius Drake in his attempts to commit sacrilege on the tomb of King Tsk VI. A tomb, incidentally, that we have no assurance even exists."

"Who is this Imperius Drake? Is he a figment of that gigantic Bear's imagination? I don't know any Imperius Drake."

"Effendi, you are in serious trouble and your lies and protests are only making things worse. We have witnesses who will swear you have been with the mad Duck and his Baboon cohort. We know that you arranged the purchase of equipment for this excursion and introduced him to Hyena, the so-called antiquarian who, like you, is available for any crime provided the price is right. And, oh yes, we have your bag with its store of documents, copious amounts of cash, several weapons and a papyrus or two for good luck. Where were you going when you were apprehended?"

"Back to Cairo. I was here in Siwa to facilitate the arrival of a group of tourists."

"The only 'tourists' you were here to 'facilitate' were the crazy Duck and his Baboon hooligan. Now, if you persist in denying your affiliation with them, you are going back to Cairo in police custody. We have enough evidence to make incarceration stick. You know how I feel about tomb robbers."

"I am not a tomb robber!!"

"Maybe not literally in this case but what would you call an attempt to reanimate a mummified Pharaoh?"

"Who told you that?"

"We have a remarkable source who has been keeping us aware of the threats you represent. You would not want to meet her."

"Her? Her? There are no females involved in our work."

"True, but nevertheless she has made herself involved. Enough of this. Where is the Duck?"

"Here in Siwa. On the other side of the oasis."

Octavius shambled over. Ignoring Effendi, he said to the Major. "There's a nasty sand storm on its way. I suggest you ride it out with us here on the Ursa Major. They are towing us to the far side of the airport where there are no buildings, aircraft or other structures that could cause damage from flying debris. We thought about taking off but we are not certain what we would have to return to. As it is, we'll probably have to plow ourselves out. We keep a snowplow on board for our winter excursions. Never thought we'd use it in the desert but…"

"I guess I don't have much choice. Effendi will just have to wait for his trip to Cairo."

# Chapter Thirty Five

## *Outside the House Outside Siwa Oasis*

*Dromedary's a wonderful breed*
*For our two desert outlaws in need.*
*Kemal is his name.*
*Transportation's his game.*
*So the search for their truck will succeed.*

Bigg and Hyena stood in the street trying to figure out which way Effendi may have gone. The desert road they had used to come to the house was to the east. The Vulture probably would have retraced their route on his first leg back to Cairo. Besides, there seemed to be more houses and buildings in that direction. They needed to find some way other than walking to search for the fugitive. He was probably far away by now but they still needed to make the effort.

Up ahead was a field with several vehicles parked somewhat at random. A tall structure that looked like a garage was off to the side. A weather beaten sign announced that this was the home of **Ships of the Desert Transport.** Just what they needed! Bigg ran on ahead and banged on the door of the building. Hyena took up the rear and arrived just as a large dromedary camel poked his nose out of an adjoining window.

"No need to break the door down! I am Kemal, sole owner and proprietor of **Ships of the Desert Transport.** Since both of you are on foot, I assume you have need of my services. No assignment too large or small. We rent by the hour, day, week, month or outright sale. Drive yourself or we provide a driver. Now, how can we address your requirements?"

Bigg blurted, "We need to find Effendi!!"

"Who, pray, is Effendi?"

"The vulture who stole our truck!"

Seeing that this dialogue would probably lead nowhere, Hyena interrupted. "Effendi is or was a partner of ours. In the middle of the night he made off with our only transportation. We are searching for him and more importantly, the return of our vehicle."

The camel emerged from the garage. "Do you have any idea where he might have gone? What was he driving?"

"A utility vehicle with a trailer hitch. We think he's on his way to Cairo."

"I assume you do not want to involve the police in this."

"No. We'll handle this ourselves."

"You are aware that a warning has been issued for a serious sandstorm. It should arrive here in the next few hours. No wheeled vehicle will be safe when it comes."

Bigg started jumping up and down. "What do we do? What do we do?"

"Fortunately, my simian friend, a partial solution is at hand. I have a utility transport that will take us safely through the desert without relying on roads. It can also turn back for shelter well before the heavy winds begin."

Hyena shook his head. "What is this miracle vehicle?"

"The original Ship of the Desert, namely, me! For a substantial consideration, I will allow you to ride upon my back as we search for your former friend. It will probably be a fool's errand," he said, staring at Bigg.

Bigg, oblivious as usual, immediately tried to jump on the dromedary's back.

"Not so fast, Baboon. I will require payment in advance and I must fetch a saddle that will accommodate the two of you. I will keep my smart phone active to keep up with the latest storm reports."

After an exchange of currency, Hyena and Bigg helped put the saddle on the camel's back and then as he knelt, they scrambled up. Bigg grabbed the pommel while Hyena grabbed Bigg.

"Are we ready? I'm going to stand up."

Hyena almost slipped off when Bigg shifted in his seat. "Baboon, I am not eager to find myself face down in the sand. Can't you settle in?"

Ignoring him, Bigg shouted, "Let's go, Kemal. We need to find that truck and that traitor, Effendi."

"I'll stay on the road as long as I can." His long, loping strides bounced his two passengers rhythmically front to back, side to side.

Hyena mumbled, "I think I'm going to be seasick."

As they exited the oasis and headed east, the morning sky was getting darker. "That sandstorm is moving this way pretty rapidly. I'll check the latest report. (Pause) It's about an hour away. We will soon be at the point of no return and I intend to return and batten down my establishment."

Bigg screamed, "Wait! Over there! In that ditch! It's the truck!" He tried to jump off the camel's back but Hyena held on to him. They moved over to the vehicle lying on its side. "Can we get it upright? Can we drive it? Where's Effendi? What happened?"

"I would guess your friend had an accident and decided to proceed on foot. Wait, he's a vulture, isn't he? He probably just flew away. Who knows where he is? Let's look inside the storage area. If there's a rope or chain, I may be able to pull it upright while you push but make it quick. That storm is coming."

Inside the truck's storage compartment were a couple of ropes that were intended for scaling walls. Hyena and Bigg tied them onto the side of the truck that was facing downward and then flipped them over the top to the camel. He in turn secured them tightly to his saddle.

"At the count of three, I'll pull and you lift and push. One, two, three!"

The truck slid across the sand. "You're going to have to lift more than push. Let's try it again"

This time the truck rotated and the two pushed it back into a vertical position.

"Now let's see if this thing is drivable. Your friend conveniently left the key when he scrammed."

Miracle of miracles. The engine coughed and started up. The wheels seemed to be in general alignment and none of the tires had burst or gone flat. Bigg gingerly put the gear shift in drive and the truck started to move.

Kemal looked at them and said, "OK, if you think you get that thing back to your site, let's give it a go. Move the ropes around and I'll tow it onto the road."

A few minutes later, a strange procession made its way back to the camel's garage. "Do you want to leave it with me until after the storm passes? I can have one of my mechanics give it a once over. What are you guys doing out here anyway?"

Before Bigg could blow their cover, Hyena said, "We're freelance explorers searching for ruins. The Antiquities Commission has given us permission to go on a search. Never know what we'll come upon."

The camel wasn't sure he bought all that but what the hell...it was none of his business. He knelt down. "All right, get back on my saddle and I'll

210

take you back to your quarters. But be quick about it. By the way, any repairs to the truck will cost you extra."

# Chapter Thirty Six

## *Inside the Ursa Major*

*As the sand and the storm rages through,*
*There are plenty of things we must do.*
*While the winds fiercely blow*
*Get drones ready to go.*
*And the choppers all set to fly, too.*

The team watched the sky turn a dark and ominous yellow as whirling cones of dust rose and fell over the airport. Then came the incessant patter of grains of sand raining down on the C-5A. The drumming increased in volume as larger clouds enveloped the ship. Inside, the twins were frightened and to be honest, so were the rest of us. The wings of the giant craft rocked and groaned. I have watched tornados whip through the Midwest US and lived through a typhoon on Mauritius. This was different. Instead of rain and steady howling winds, we were being showered repeatedly with loads of dirt, debris and even mud caused by the sand being mixed with standing water. One big plus. The storm was moving through rapidly, transforming the landscape as it went. Covering and uncovering! Shaping and reshaping!

Major Akil and Effendi were old hands at riding out dust storms. The rest of us were not. While we were taken up with the tempest, the Mau was giving the Vulture a different kind of pelting – question after question!

"We know about Imperius Drake and his history of wild and dangerous capers. He tried to assassinate the entire professional genetics community in Las Vegas. He destroyed a priceless sapphire in the process. He has a long standing vendetta against Octavius Bear. He has cheated thousands out of major sums of money with his fraudulent investment schemes. His deadly egg-shaped weapon - The Black Quack – has nearly killed and certainly wounded hundreds. Each one of his activities gets wilder and wilder. Why is he trying to re-animate the mummy of King Tsk VI, assuming it exists and he can find it?"

"I don't know."

"Of course you know. You wouldn't agree to assist him if you didn't have detailed knowledge of his plans. You're much too cautious to be blindsided by an insane menace like this Duck. He must have paid you quite well. We have proof of some of your ill-gotten gains from the contents of your bag. We also know about the Ground Penetrating Radar and other equipment you rented for him."

During this inquisition, Octavius had rejoined them. "I assume he has one or more versions of the Portable Endoatmospheric Particle Beam Projector."

"The what?'

"The Ray Gun! How do you think he's going to excavate around the tomb without a large team of laborers and equipment? The gun will do it for him. His crony, Bigg Baboon, for all his stupidity, is an excellent shot with it. He'll use it as a tool and a formidable weapon. Fortunately, we have several units with us. Imperius stole an early model and plans from my labs at Universal Ursine Industries. We've upgraded our models and I can only assume Imperius has done the same. Now, back to the Major's question. Why does he want to re-animate the Pharaoh?"

"All right! He doesn't want the King. He wants his guards and army. He's raving about world conquest through an inexhaustible supply of cloned ghost warriors subservient to his will. The Pharaoh is his agent of access to them. But then the Duck will dispose of the King after the warriors have switched their allegiance to himself. That's all I know."

"What's the Hyena's role in all this?"

"His job is to read and activate the Pharaoh's Book of the Dead. According to the Duck, there is no papyrus version of funerary texts. They believe the coffin and surrounding constructions actually contain the Book. Hyena is to locate and figure this out and invoke the protective spirits to re-animate and liberate the King."

The Major whistled. "Now, there's a crackpot scheme if I ever heard one. Actually, if anyone could pull it off, Hyena is probably the best candidate. OK! Where are they?"

"In a large house on the other side of the oasis. Let me go and I'll show it to you."

"What do you think. Doctor Bear?"

"Let's do it in reverse, Major. Effendi, as soon as this storm is over, we'll put you in a helicopter and you can lead us there. Then we'll think about letting you loose. I'm sure the Major can find you again, if he needs to. We'll keep your documents."

The winds had died down considerably and the view from the Ursa Major's cockpit was unimpeded. Colonel Where cracked open the crew access door and climbed down. Sand covered the landing gear but little else seemed to be immersed. The giant craft's wings must have served as an umbrella. Whatever sand was on top of the wings could be shaken off by movement. From what he could see, the airport's runway was in deep sand in places and several stanchions were bent over. The buildings seemed to be intact. He went back inside the plane and descended into the hold.

"It looks like we lucked out, Octavius. No damage that I can see and the covers on the engines held. We're going to have to give all the control surfaces a good going over and testing."

"Do you think we can get one of the helicopters out and airworthy, Colonel? We're going to need it to track down the Duck."

"It'll take us a couple of hours to refit the rotors but after that, we'll be good to go. Do you know where he is?"

"No, but our good friend Effendi does and he's going to lead us there. In the meantime, let's send out a drone and survey the area."

Frau Schuylkill trotted off toward the drone control bay as the mechanics set the little craft up on the forward ramp, fueled it and checked out its controls. "We're set up, Frau."

Octavius, Inspector Wallaroo, the Colonel and I joined her in the control bay. First images of the airport. Some cleanup necessary to get the ramps and runway back but no apparent structural damage. The tower looked OK. Lots of activity! The Frau set a course following the perimeter road that encircled the oasis. Vehicles off to the side. Several palm trees toppled over onto the roadway. In one area, a major sand dune had arisen in the middle of what had been an outdoor bazaar. Some houses were surrounded by a couple of feet of sand.

Octavius called to the Major and Effendi. "Maybe we won't have to take you for a ride, Vulture. You know this oasis and you probably rented the house they're staying in. Look at the console as we move around the perimeter. Do you see them?"

"No, I don't."

"Continue the scan, Frau Ilse. Wait! Hold it there. Let the drone hover. Close up on that house with the truck in the courtyard."

I looked closely at the screen. "There's a camel, some sort of dog and…a baboon. Octavius, I'd swear that's Bigg and that dog may be a hyena. No idea who the camel is. Colonel, is that the truck Effendi was driving when you captured him?"

"It sure looks like it and it's banged up a bit on one side. I guess the camel helped them right it again. OK, Effendi, let's have some truth here."

"All right, that's the house and the truck. I don't know who the camel is. He might be a repair beast."

The Colonel looked over at Octavius and the Major. "What do you want to do? The chopper should be ready in another hour or so. We could just fly over and haul them in."

The Great Bear snorted, "And charge them with what? No. The Major and I want to catch them in the act and make it stick. But we need to keep strict tabs on them. How much longer can we keep the drone on station?"

The Frau looked up. "About five more hours. I'll send out the second drone in time to retrieve this one."

# Chapter Thirty Seven

## *Outside the House Outside Siwa Oasis*

*When Imperius goes on a rage,*
*It's a frenzy you cannot assuage.*
*With a new truck in hand,*
*He screams out at his band*
*And announces the fight they will wage.*

The wind had subsided but Imperius had not. Envision a jet black Duck throwing a hissy fit. He raged against the sandstorm. He seethed against the traitorous Effendi. He fulminated at the delays in mounting his world shattering project. He fumed at the inefficiencies of the Baboon and the cavalier attitude of the Hyena. But he reserved his most explosive wrath for that odious ursine, Octavius Bear. He had noticed the drone passing overhead and was certain it was searching for him. The Police, the Army or this most probable, his arch enemy, the Kodiak Klutz.

"Baboon, get the ray gun and shoot that flying snoop out of the sky!"

The Hyena interrupted. "Not a good idea, Imperius. You'll only confirm the fact that we are here and we are on the defensive. That drone can't stay up there forever. When it moves, we should move. By the way, do you have any idea where you want to go? "

"I have flown around the area since the storm ended. It may be too much to hope for but I believe some of the sands shifted and a partial shape

218

similar to a mastaba has surfaced. We must get there with all speed. Is the truck drivable, Baboon? We need to have the Ground Penetrating Radar at the ready."

"The camel has to do some repairs on the steering. It'll take most of the morning."

"Does he have another vehicle we can rent?"

"I dunno. I suppose so. That's his business."

"Well, idiot, go and find out. But be careful, don't let them see you from the drone."

It wasn't at all clear to Bigg exactly how this trick of elusive maneuvering was to be carried out but he knew if he asked or argued with the Duck, it would just result in more noise, heat and fluttering feathers. Bigg was getting awfully tired of this whole scheme and he was getting even more tired of Imperius. He needed to figure out a way of getting away like Effendi did. Or…or perhaps there was another more permanent solution to the problem.

Placing a blanket over his head and body, he dashed out the door toward Kemal's *Ships of the Desert Transport* garage and parking lot. Out of breath, he ran into the building, then turned and peeked out at the sky. The drone was nowhere to be seen. It was probably still on station over the house.

The camel strode over from his office and said, "Strange keffiyeh you're wearing! Looks more like a blanket. Your truck is just about ready but I wouldn't push it too hard. I had to use substitute parts on the steering linkage."

219

Bigg shrugged and said, "Do you have a sturdier truck we can rent? It has to have a trailer hitch. We need it to go to the archeology site."

"Considering what happened to your truck, I'm reluctant to let you rent one of mine. However, I can sell you one that's more powerful and definitely in much better shape."

"How much?" The haggling began and ended with Bigg driving away with a light military vehicle. As he approached the house, slipping and sliding through the displaced sand, he noticed a cluster of palm trees that had stood up to the winds. He parked in their shadows and bounded the rest of the way back to the house.

Imperius was still in High Dudgeon. *(A small village that catered to sociopaths.)* "Well, what have you got, Baboon? I will not be kept from my appointment with destiny."

Wondering who Destiny was, Bigg replied, "I bought a truck that can pull the trailer through the sand. Where are we going?"

"I cannot fly around with that drone overhead but I estimate our target is only a few kilometers away. We must wait until that aerial menace disappears and then drive like mad into the desert."

Although driving like mad was the Baboon's specialty, he wondered if Hyena was a skilled driver. Hyena would have to drive if Bigg was going to operate the Ground Penetrating Radar. He looked up again and this time the drone had disappeared. He ran over to the palm trees, jumped in the truck,

220

drove it to the courtyard and started hitching up the trailer. "Hyena, give me a paw here. Let's get this show on the road."

Imperius emerged and once again, eschewing anything that smacked of manual labor, began screaming for them to load up and go. Bigg had already transferred the contents of the original truck. *(He wasn't sure what Effendi had taken with him when he abandoned the overturned vehicle. Little did they know that Effendi and his loot were in the hands of the Great Bear.)* The Duck half leapt and half flew into the cab, shouting for them to hurry.

"Time is of the essence. I must know if the storm swept the sand from the mastaba. Do you have the radar and the guns, Baboon?"

Bigg nodded and told Hyena to take the driver's seat. He would sit in the back and keep tabs on the trailer.

"Where are we going, Imperius?"

The Duck pulled a GPS display out of a knapsack and after staring at it for a few moments, shouted. "West. We must head West! I have carefully plotted the coordinates of what I am sure is the tomb site."

"How do you know that?" they both asked.

"I have studied the ancient writings as well as the reports of previous expeditions who failed. But I will profit from their failures. Careful analysis and unerring measurement will prove its value. I stand on the threshold of a greatness never before known. Imperius Drake is about to become Supreme Lord of the Universe."

Hyena, even more convinced that he was dealing with a Supreme Crackpot, nodded and resumed refining his plans for ditching the Duck in the desert along with the idiot Baboon. He would have been surprised to know that at that moment, Bigg was doing the same. Bigg really didn't care what happened to Hyena but he had to get away from Imperius. He was sure that once Imperius' plan for conquest took place, he would no longer be needed. The Duck would have an entire army at his beck and call. No room for a Baboon. Imperius might even try to have him killed. Bigg would have to make sure Imperius didn't raise the Pharaoh from the Dead. Maybe the best way to stop that would be to kill off Hyena. He needed to think. *(A very difficult task for Bigg.)*

# Chapter Thirty Eight

## *In and Around the Ursa Major*

*The scared vulture decides to take flight*
*And he gives everyone a great fright.*
*He grabs one little bear.*
*Carries her through the air*
*And he ditches her far out of sight.*

"They are on the move, Herr Bear!" Frau Schuylkill looked up from the drone control display. "They are heading west. They have a new truck and the equipment trailer is hooked up to it. As best I can tell, the Duck, Hyena and Baboon are on board. I'm operating from a high enough altitude and keeping the sun behind the drone so they will not be aware that we are tracking them. I do not have any weapons on the drone or I would attempt to stop them right there."

"No Frau, I want to let them get to their excavation site. If they truly know where the King's tomb is, we want to share in that knowledge. Colonel, is at least one of the helicopters good to go?"

"We're running tests as we speak, Octavius. So far, so good! Give us another half hour."

"If they're running through the desert with a trailer in tow, they're not going to set any speed records. Besides, they have to find the place and dig out the tomb. We have no idea how long any of that will take. I'm sure he'll try to use the radar and ray gun. I doubt Hyena has any excavation skills and Imperius will not dirty his wings and claws. That leaves Bigg. Actually, he's proven himself a pretty good shot with the gun but I don't know about the Ground Penetrating Radar. Effendi! Do yourself a favor and tell us what you know about the Duck's plans."

The Vulture replied, "Imperius is convinced he knows where the site is. I don't know where. I also have no idea what effect the sandstorm had. The mastaba could be exposed. It could be buried under tons of sand. I still don't think it even exists."

Major Akil spoke up. "That won't keep us from prosecuting you for aiding and abetting tomb robbery. Unauthorized attempts at discovering, entering, disturbing and removing artifacts are severely punished nowadays. I'm not even sure what the penalty is for attempting to re-animate a mummy. I don't think the officials who drafted the laws even saw that as possibility. But we'll think of something. I've been waiting for a long time to catch up with you and Hyena. I'm not going to let you slip through my paws again."

This left Effendi with only one course of action. Escape!! He would need a diversion. There were several light trucks stored in the cargo bay of the C-5A. When they opened the front hatch to roll out the helicopter, he would drive one of the trucks down the ramp and block it. Then he could fly off on his own power before they had a chance to chase him down. But the first thing he had to do was untie the knots that held his legs together. They hadn't tried to secure his wings. Stupid of them!

At last, when no one was looking, he hobbled out of the cargo container they had dumped him in and rubbed the ropes against a sharp structural beam on the side of the fuselage. Success! He was free!

The technicians were opening the forward hatch. Now for a truck to block the ramp before they could move the helicopter out. Suddenly a better idea struck him. He needed a hostage. One of the bear cubs. Light enough for him to lift and still fly. They were sitting next to the little dog Nanny watching the hatch open. She might make a better victim but no, the cubs were more important. He would swoop down and grab one and fly out of the hatch. If they tried to pursue him with the chopper, he would threaten to drop the cub from a great height. Otherwise, he would deposit the little bear in the desert and let them search while he escaped.

One of the cubs got up to get a closer look at the final work being done on the helicopter's rotors. Now was his chance. With a thump of his wings, he took flight, headed for the open hatch, grabbing the struggling cub in his claws.

"Momma, Poppa, help!" It was Arabella.

Confident that they couldn't follow him with the chopper, Effendi flew a straight line to the east, holding on tightly to the wriggling cub. He didn't want to kill her. He had enough charges against him already. He soared out over the open desert, looking for a spot to leave her that would chew up their resources looking for her. He wheeled down over a steep sand dune and coming close to the ground, let go of his hostage. He turned to watch the little bear pick herself up and start running up the side of the dune. Then he rose up

225

into higher altitudes. He had made his getaway. He didn't notice the shadow moving up on him. He had forgotten about Condo. Bad mistake!

Large as vultures may grow, they are no match for an Andean condor. Condo had taken off after them and was waiting to see if Effendi would release Arabella unharmed. He did. Making a note of the cub's location, he called back to the Ursa Major, giving them directions to rescue her. Then with several flaps of his twelve foot wings, he overtook the vulture and power dived on top of him knocking him spiraling into the ground.

L. Condor flew low to observe his victim. The impact had broken the vulture's neck. Too bad. He could have been more helpful. Oh well! The police could pick up the body. Time to get back to Arabella.

He found the cub slipping and sliding on the side of the steep dune. He landed next to her. Arabella shrieked. Then she realized that the vulture had not come back. This was Uncle Condo. He gently picked her up, flapped his wings and there she was sitting on top of the dune.

"Is he gone, Uncle Condo?"

"Yes, he is, little one. He won't be bothering you or anyone else anymore. Are you all right?"

"I have a few scratches from his claws but otherwise, I'm OK. Oh, I was so scared. I was sure he was going to drop me from the sky."

"Well, you're safe now. We'll wait for your momma and poppa to come with the helicopter. One ride in a bird's claws is enough for a day."

Back at the C-5A, pandemonium had broken out. Mlle Woof was having a fit of hysterics. She had failed to keep Arabella safe. Belinda was comforting McTavish who was sure he'd never see his sister again. Octavius was pushing the tech crew to finish getting the helicopter airworthy. The Flying Tigers were standing by to take it out and find Arabella. The Colonel and I were keeping contact with Condo. Frau Schuylkill was controlling the drones, tracking Imperius, Bigg and Hyena in their truck. Otto and Chita were trying to calm Mlle Woof down. Major Akil was issuing orders to the local and Antiquities police to be on the lookout for Effendi and his captive.

Then we heard from Condo. Arabella was safe. Effendi was dead. They would wait for the helicopter. For the moment, getting Arabella back had top priority over Imperius. The Major called in the coordinates where Effendi's body was to be found by the police.

Sighs of relief all around except for Mlle Woof who was devastated. She was certain that she had failed in her duties. Belinda took her aside and tried to convince her that nobody held her responsible. Everyone believed the cubs were quite safe inside the plane. As to her thinking she had failed, it was quite the contrary. Octavius and she were delighted with the dog's care and concern and her skills in keeping the cubs in tow and learning so rapidly and well. There was never any thought of the Bichon resigning. They wouldn't hear of it.

Somewhat mollified, she went over to Octavius and again apologized and was again reassured. Then she and McTavish went and sat on the forward ramp awaiting the return of the helicopter and Arabella. Condo had gone back to keeping station over Effendi's body until the police arrived.

227

Finally, the sound of rotors cut through the now windless atmosphere and a major crowd gathered to welcome the cub back into the fold. No longer shaken by her experience, she bounced from the chopper's cabin and ran first to her mother, then Octavius and then her brother and Mlle Woof. Now that Arabella was safe, McTavish was convinced he would be hearing about her flirtation with death "ad nauseum." Mlle Woof apologized profusely to her young charge, who simply embraced her and told her there was nothing to apologize for.

Then the Frau cut the celebration short by announcing that Imperius had stopped in a deserted valley and was taking up what looked like a working position and campsite.

"Well," said the Great Bear, "looks like it's time to get our act together. Condo, Arabella, McTavish, we need to talk with Raamjet again. Call her on your game consoles."

The cubs ran to the storage bay where their two game consoles were installed. "Uncle Condo, hook us in!! We have to talk to her right away."

"Just a moment, little ones. Patience is not a bear cub virtue. All right, log in."

Click, click, click, tap, tap, tap! "You messed up the password. Do it again!"

More clicks, more taps! Ta-da! Success!

"Raamjet, it's us! Arabella and McTavish. Poppa needs to talk with you right now! Come out, come out, wherever you are!"

Twin red lights glowed and slowly filled the screens. The Uraeus was there. Her piercing eyes unblinking in the dark. "Greetings, young friends. It has been a while since we spoke. Where is the Seeker of Justice?"

A deep throated rumble echoed in the storage bay. "Greetings, O Protector of the Tomb. We have news. Our mutual nemesis is taking action. We suspect that he has found what he thinks is the King's mastaba. We are watching him and his underlings with our aerial observation platform. Do you sense anything?"

"No, but he will be greeted appropriately if he trespasses. I cannot perceive the outside world in which you and he reside but once he tries to enter my domain, I will deal with him.

# Chapter Thirty Nine

## *At the Site???*

*Things are getting progressively bad.*
*It's a nightmare like none of them had.*
*The Hyena and Bigg*
*Are reluctant to dig.*
*Is Imperius stark, raving mad?*

"This is the place. I am certain of it. Baboon, get out the radar and the guns. We will dig here."

Hyena was unconvinced as was Bigg. "What makes you so sure? No one has dug here before. Who is your source of information?"

'The Pharaoh himself, you fools! I have been in contact with him many times. He wishes to be revivified and rule once again. I have him convinced that I will be his faithful vizier and restore him and his armies to a full living state. He knows nothing of my true plans."

"You and the King have been communicating? How?"

"In dreams! I will tell you no more than that!"

Now the hyena and baboon were utterly convinced they were dealing with a psycho. Bigg took Hyena to the side and said, "He takes a serum that alters his personality. I think it finally got to him."

"Perhaps it's better if we humor him. There is still a profit to be made with this expedition, as you well know. With Effendi gone, there is more for us." (*Little did Hyena know that Effendi was gone permanently.*)

"And,' thought Bigg, "with you gone there will be more for me. I'll wait but not for long. There may be treasure in the tomb. If there really is a tomb."

He turned to the trailer and started hauling out the GPR. "Which way? All I see is sand."

"That is because, as usual, Baboon, you have no vision. Fortunately, I have more than enough for this task. Aim at that dune over there."

With Hyena's help, Bigg got the radar set up and began making test sweeps to calibrate the device. The Duck kept urging him on. "Hurry, Baboon, hurry. The Pharaoh is waiting. What do you see? What do you see?"

"Sand!"

"Go nearer and aim deeper!"

"Sand!"

"Incompetent! Can you do nothing right?"

While Bigg was not gifted with a great intellect, he was endowed with a furious temper. He kicked the carriage of the radar display. "You do it! If you're so smart. Take the handle bars. See if you can find anything."

Normally, Imperius would have been taken aback by the Baboon's rebellious behavior. But he was so intent on looking for the tomb that he gave little notice to the changed Bigg. He would regret it. Recognizing that he was not physically configured to handle the radar and its cart, he turned to Hyena and said, "You handle it. I will guide you."

Hyena was none too pleased with the arrangement, especially since it left Bigg in control of the guns. This whole process was showing signs of getting completely out of control. He looked over at the sulking Baboon and then tentatively took up the radar's handle bars, aiming the unit's probe in the direction Imperius had pointed. At first nothing! Then a shadow on the screen indicating a solid formation under the sand. He amplified the signal and moved along a track meeting the source of the reflection. Sure enough, the image was becoming more defined. Could it be the mastaba or just a rocky mass buried in the sand?

There was no doubt in Imperius' mind. "This is it, this is it! Baboon, bring the gun. Aim it at that pile of sand. Use a sweeping motion and clear the cover. Hurry! Be careful, Baboon! Do not damage the structure!"

Bigg put the gun on wide spectrum and released a surge of radiation at the sand dune. A rectangular shape began to appear.

The Baboon resisted the urge to fire the gun at the Duck and continued to clear the sand away while Hyena wrestled with the radar cart. Imperius rushed back and forth, searching the radar's screen and then shouting more orders at Bigg. As the sand further disintegrated, a limestone box about 30 meters (ninety feet) across emerged. This was no outcropping of rock. It was symmetrical. It was a building of some sort.

"The mastaba! The mastaba! The mastaba!" the duck shouted over and over.

Hyena looked up from the GPR screen and said, "It certainly is an edifice of some kind but how do we know it's the Pharaoh's tomb?"

Imperius would brook no disagreement. "Your role, Hyena, is to positively assist in this great project. I will hear no more negativity from either of you. Now, let us find the entrance. Use the radar."

The baboon and hyena wrestled the GPR onto the roof of the low lying structure and proceeded to walk off its dimensions. Several chambers connected by tunnels appeared on the screen but they went extremely deep. If this was indeed the tomb of Tsk VI, he was buried far beneath the limestone façade. Reaching him was going to be a major undertaking.

# Chapter Forty

## *At the Ursa Major*

*With Octavius' team standing by*
*While the first drone continues to spy.*
*One more chat with the snake.*
*Everyone wide awake.*
*And a chopper is ready to fly.*

All of this activity was being carefully transmitted back by the drone. Frau Ilse shouted out. "Herr Bear, they have uncovered something. It looks like a ceremonial building. It could be a tomb."

The team clustered around the drone control station. The cubs jumped up on their parents' shoulders and Bruce Wallaroo just jumped.

"Colonel, is the helicopter ready to go?"

"Yes! I have it on standby. The second bird will be ready in another hour."

"Well, let's keep it that way. We don't yet know what they found and if we are going to charge them with something, we need to determine whether it is actually the Pharaoh's mastaba. Major Akil, what's your opinion?"

"As the Frau says, it looks like a ceremonial building but it could be anything. The odds are quite good that if it is a tomb, the burial chambers will be far underground with traps and dead ends to foil tomb robbers. If the history is reliable, the priests and royal court would have taken careful steps to ensure this King stays safely buried away. No one wanted him or his armies resurrected. Oddly enough, belief in the Underworld and the likelihood of return of the dead were widely accepted during that period. That may explain the removal of the brain and vital organs during mummification. I think we should watch and wait. But not too long."

Octavius looked around. "Any other opinions, contrary or not?"

Belinda squinted and sighed. "I think we need to call Raamjet again."

"Absolutely! OK, kids and Condo. Let's get the Uraeus on the line. If it is a tomb and the right tomb, she needs to know ASAP."

Scampering over to the video hookup, once again the little ambassadors to the Underworld called up the snake. "We have news! We have news! The nasty Duck has found a tomb!"

Belinda cut them off saying, "Imperius and his cohorts have unearthed a building. We don't yet know what it is. Do you sense their presence?"

"I sense nothing as of yet. The burial chamber is deep underground and I have only a virtual presence in it. I will first note them when their spirits manifest themselves. I am in contact with you through the same virtual channels."

"Then how can you do battle with them, armed as they are with powerful material weapons?"

"I will attack their souls."

"But you are physical, aren't you? Can they harm you?"

"I do have a corporeal aspect and perhaps they can do me damage. We shall see but I have significant resources. If indeed they reach the tomb and try to read the incantations of the Book of the Dead inscribed on the King's catafalque and coffin, I will know and I will act."

"Meanwhile, said Belinda, "we will be coming after them on the material level. We are waiting to see if indeed it is the Pharaoh's tomb they have found. Judging from their actions, they seem to think so but the mad Duck is perpetually confident of his own judgement. He is usually wrong. As this progresses, we will be in constant contact.with you."

"I thank you, Noble Consort of the Justice Seeker. I am greatly indebted to all of you and especially to you, young ursine sprites. Farewell for the moment."

"Momma, what are sprites?"

"Mischievous little creatures!"

236

# Chapter Forty One

## At _THE_ Tomb??

_Is this strange structure really a tomb?_
_And if so, it's intended for whom?_
_It's a puzzling thing._
_Can it be for the King?_
_Is his mummy in some deep, dark room?_

"It is the tomb! It is the tomb!" Imperius flew back and forth over the partially uncovered limestone, flapping his wings and generally getting in the way of Bigg and Hyena.

Just about at his limit, Hyena shouted at the Duck, "It is _A_ tomb. It may or may not be for Tsk VI or any Pharaoh. It could be a priest or an official of the court or a dead wife or queen. We have no idea of its date or provenance. We need to gain access and sort these things out."

"Well, do it! Do it! Quickly! Quickly!" Baboon, remove all the sand! Hyena, find the entrance! I will tolerate no delays or mistakes. Now! Now! Now!"

Convinced the Duck had completely lost it, Bigg fired the ray gun at Imperius… and missed.

"Be careful, you idiot! You almost hit me. Concentrate on removing the sand." It would never have occurred to the Duck that Bigg intended to deliberately shoot him. His supreme confidence in his domination over the

237

Baboon and his total disregard for Bigg's feelings and intelligence *(such as it was)* blinded him totally to any potential peril.

A shout from Hyena. "This looks like an entrance. Let's check it on the radar!"

"No time for that, Baboon, blast it open and Hyena, get inside!"

"What, and fall into a deep pit. Imperius, these ancients were no dummies. They built these things to resist tomb robbers and other invaders. I'm going nowhere until we check it out. The obvious entrance is probably a trap."

Imperius could understand deviousness when he came upon it. Hyena was probably right. It's the way he would have designed a tomb. Traps, diversions and dead-ends. "All right, do your checking but be quick about it. Baboon, clear the rest of the sand away. We will have to examine the entire structure. Delays, delays!"

The radar images were insufficient. A coffin or chamber would normally appear as a monolith or opening without giving much detail as to its contents. Tunnels and passages show depth and direction but give little indication of the stability of the walls and ceilings. In short, individual "in situ" surveying is still necessary to determine the presence, nature and accessibility of the funereal chambers. This takes time.

The Baboon continued to spray the surface of the structure with wide band bursts, dissolving the sand but leaving the limestone intact. How he managed this delicate maneuver wasn't quite clear to any of them including

Bigg but it was working. Of course, this was totally beyond the Duck's ability to appreciate.

On the far side of the mastaba, the limestone turned color. A large rectangle of darker hue emerged. Could this be the entry point? Imperius thought so. "Bring the radar! Bring the radar!" Hyena jockeyed the cart into position over the darkened space. The screen showed a complex image of openings and tunnels.

"This is it!" shouted the Duck. "Baboon, blast it open."

Imperius grabbed the gun out of Bigg's paws and fired a shot at the center of the rectangle. The limestone cover collapsed inward, revealing a wide staircase cut into what looked like solid rock. Brandishing a high powered flash light, Imperius jumped into the void. His voiced echoed back. "Follow me! Follow me! Quickly! Quickly!"

Needless to say, neither Hyena nor Bigg were all that eager to comply.

# Chapter Forty Two

## *Aboard the Ursa Major*

*Now it's time to get on with the show.*
*We pursuers are ready to go.*
*The mad Duck is inside*
*So we must turn the tide.*
*We must deal him a heart stopping blow.*

"Herr Bear," growled Frau Schuylkill, gazing at the drone display console, "they have opened the tomb. The verdammt Duck is inside. What are your orders?"

Octavius turned to Major Akil and said, "I think we now have an actionable situation. He's entered an antique site. We have no definite identification of who or what is inside but the structure is definitely ancient."

The cat hissed and said, "All right! I think we have enough evidence to pull him in. How do we get there?"

Octavius shouted, "Colonel are the choppers ready?"

"Good to go, Octavius."

"OK, I want you, Otto, Condo and Chita in the first ship. I'll take the second with Maury, Bruce, the Major and his helicopter pilot. We'll meet up on the site. Make sure each team has a fully charged particle projector and other side arms. We'll probably need digging tools and plenty of lights. Frau Schuylkill, I'd like you to stay on the drone consoles to continue to guide us and keep surveillance on the mastaba."

Belinda approached and said, "Tavi. you'll never fit inside those tunnels. Why don't you stay back here at the command post?"

"I know. Although, the Pharaoh was a hippo. They must have created some passages large enough to accommodate his bulk. Assuming, that is, that this is his tomb. I wonder how Imperius can be so certain. Anyway, I want to be there when they flush him out. It will take several of us to subdue him, Bigg and the Hyena."

"They have at least one ray gun. Maybe more. And what will you do if he rouses the King's army?"

"We can't let him get that far. You're also forgetting about Raamjet. If this is the correct tomb, she will be ready for the Duck's invasion. We need to make contact with her. Will you handle that and keep us posted? I'm also counting on you and Mlle Woof to protect the cubs here in the Ursa Major."

"That goes without saying, Tavi. I just don't want you doing anything foolish. We both know that screwy Duck is just about capable of anything. How many times did we think he was dead?"

"At least twice and maybe more. This time I will have no scruples at all in dealing with him and his thug assistant. I know the team feels the same way. Once he was simply a challenge. Now he's an extremely dangerous cosmic threat and has to be permanently stopped. I'm on my way."

Belinda shook her head and headed back to the twins and Mlle Woof. "Come on, little ones. We have to talk with Raamjet."

The cubs ran to the game consoles and logged on. L. Condor had added a few features that made it easier to call Raamjet. It wasn't clear what device, if any, the snake used to communicate with them so they turned on the new search and hail feature and called the name of the Uraeus. Two juvenile bear voices echoed through the halls of the Underworld over and over.

"Raamjet, Raamjet, it's us. (Yes, Momma! We know. *It's we*.) Poppa is on his way to the tomb with his team. We think that nasty Duck has found it. Come and talk with us."

Silence and then that rustling sound accompanied by several hisses. Out of the darkness two shining rubies appeared. "I am here, young ones. Is your Lady Mother with you?"

"She's here, she's here. So is Mlle Woof."

"I greet you all. So, the Duck is proceeding with his mad adventure. We still cannot be sure that he has found the mastaba of King Tsk VI. I will not actually sense him until he tries to invoke the Pharaoh's Book of the Dead. Then he will have invaded my universe and will pay the price."

Belinda replied. "We aren't sure either, but he has found something and Octavius, his team and the Egyptian Antiquities Police have enough cause to arrest him for desecrating a sacred site. They do not want to give him a chance to actually find and invoke the Book of the Dead if one exists."

"Is it possible for me to speak directly with the Seeker of Justice?'

"He is in transit to the site. It will take a bit of adjustment here and in his helicopters but I'm sure we can connect you through these game consoles. I will make arrangements and call you back."

"I await your return. May the gods of the Underworld be with you all."

"Frau Schuylkill, can you reach Condo? We have a job for him."

# Chapter Forty Three

## At *THE* Tomb

*In a spacious but quite empty hall*
*Mad Imperius comes to a wall.*
*Is this too a dead end?*
*He is at his wit's end.*
*His two minions respond to his call*

"Bring more lights, bring more lights, you idiots!" The Duck's quacking echoed up the passageways and tunnels as he ran, slipped, fell and fluttered his way deeper and deeper until he came to a dead end. He was facing a wall of stones etched with hieroglyphs. "Hyena, come! Bring lights and Baboon, bring the gun. There is a wall blocking my way. It is covered with writing. We must get past it but first I want know what the ancients inscribed on it. Hurry!"

His two cronies picked their way along the shafts and stairs, carrying bright LED lanterns and the gun. They had left the radar up on the roof. When they got to the Duck, he screamed again.

"Where is the radar? Where is the radar? I want to see beyond this wall. Bigg, bring the radar!"

Resisting the urge to blast the Duck on the spot, Bigg shrugged and headed back up the tortuous passageways and stairs. Hyena approached the wall and began to read the inscriptions.

"What does it say? What does it say?"

"It begins with the customary warnings, curses and threats against any who would commit sacrilege by disturbing the remains of the great King Tsk VI. It goes on to list his virtues, power and accomplishments. Mostly fiction, I'm sure. Several of the priests and other functionaries are mentioned. No doubt they were the team who interred the Pharaoh. I will scan and copy it with my smart phone."

"I knew it! I knew it! He's here! He's here! Give me the gun. I will blast down this wall right now."

"Wait, Imperius! The ancients were not fools They did not issue warnings idly. If what we know about the Pharaoh is even partly true, they will have gone to great pains to ensure he could never be reached again. You don't know what lies behind this wall nor do we know if there are more messages on the other side of it. There are, no doubt, traps. We must be very cautious. Remember, we need to find the Book of the Dead if you are going on with your scheme to revivify King Tsk. It may be that the Book is not a Book at all. In some other royal tombs, the catafalque, bier and coffin were inscribed with the prayers and formulations needed for the person's successful transition to the Underworld. Destroy or deface them and your dream goes with them."

Wonder of wonders! The Duck subsided momentarily, shook his head and accepted Hyena's warning. "Well, Hyena, what do you recommend?"

"Wait till Bigg returns with the GPR. We can see what is behind this wall. If it seems safe, we can take it down stone by stone and…"

245

"Stone by stone! That will take forever!"

"Not if you put the gun on a very narrow beam and break the seal between each stone very carefully. You said that the Baboon was quite skillful in handling the rays."

"It is one of his very few talents. The other is heavy lifting. Very well, we shall follow that course after scanning this wall. Where is that confounded ape?"

On cue, Bigg came down the stairway, bouncing the radar cart in front of him.

"Be careful, you idiot. You'll disturb the settings on the probes. Bring the unit up here and aim it at the wall. We'll sweep from top to bottom."

As they watched the screen on the GPR, it became evident that there was a large space behind the wall BUT it appeared to be totally empty. It was probably some sort of anteroom. Where was the sarcophagus? Where is the Book of the Dead? Where is the mummy of the Pharaoh?

"Another trick by the ancients! All right, Let's take down the wall...stone by stone. Bigg, use the gun...carefully."

Once again the Baboon considered firing at Imperius. Once again, he changed his mind. Conflicting emotions. How would he get on living by himself? Where would he go? Would he have to kill the Hyena, too? What happened to Effendi? If he was gone, Bigg would have the Duck's fortune all to himself. Were there riches to be gotten from the mummy's case and surrounding rooms? He would wait and see.

"Baboon, use the gun!"

# Chapter Forty Four

## Enroute to __THE__ Tomb

*The Uraeus is back on the line.*
*She's describing the chambers' design.*
*How the anteroom wall*
*And the ceiling will fall*
*Killing them like a caving-in mine.*

As the two helicopters settled in near the mastaba, I thought I caught sight of Bigg pushing a bulky cart across the roof and into an opening. He obviously didn't notice the choppers.

"Hey Octavius! They're in there. I just saw Bigg pushing a cart. I think it's Ground Penetrating Radar."

"Good catch, Maury. Let's hang back and do a little strategizing. Get the team from the first chopper over here and we'll work out our approach. I don't want anyone barging in there when the Duck has the ray gun."

The chopper's com unit squawked. It was Condo in the first ship. "Octavius, the Bearoness is on the line. She wants me to patch us through to the cubs' play consoles so we can converse with Raamjet. She told the snake that Imperius had reached a tomb. Still not sure it's the right one."

"Thanks, Senhor! I think we'll assume it is the right one. Can you make the connections?"

248

"It'll take me a few minutes but I'll get it set up and then ping you. Meanwhile the Bearoness and the cubs are calling the Uraeus to join them and us."

"Good! The Major is here with me. I want him to speak with Raamjet as well."

The crew from the first ship had assembled next to the Great Bear's helicopter and Octavius was holding court.

"We all know what an unpredictable and highly dangerous nut Imperius Drake is. I don't know what to think about Bigg Baboon except he is extraordinarily short on brain power and has followed Imperius slavishly throughout their relationship. The Hyena is another story. I believe his first order of business is self-preservation. Am I correct, Major, that he is strictly a mercenary who sells his services to the highest bidder?"

"That is how we describe him, Octavius. Stealth and chicanery but he has never been aggressive or life-threatening. I'm sure he has already taken in a tidy sum for his efforts thus far. If indeed, they find the King and his Book of the Dead, it will be Hyena who will be reading the incantations. He is a charlatan but he is expert in what he does and knows. I doubt if he believes anything will result from his efforts. He is more likely to be killed off by the Duck in the face of failure than destroyed by the revivified Pharaoh and his followers. He's playing a very dangerous game. Not like him. Imperius must have promised some fabulous rewards."

Just then the copter's com unit squawked again. Condo! "I've patched in the two systems and the cubs' play stations are online. You won't be able to see Raamjet but you can speak to her and hear her."

"OK. Belinda, is the Uraeus there?"

"She is on her way."

"Hello Poppa. It's me. McTavish! Did you find the King's tomb? Is that nasty Duck there?"

"We think so, son. That's why we need to talk to Raamjet. You and Arabella behave and don't give Momma or Mlle Woof any trouble."

"Yessir. *(disappointed sound as only a bear cub can utter.)* Here's Raamjet now."

Belinda's voice rang over the ship's speakers. "I greet you again, oh Uraeus! My consort and his team are at the site of what they believe to be the King's tomb. We also believe that Imperius Drake and two of his henchbeasts are inside the structure. We have arranged a connection so you may speak directly with the Seeker of Justice. Unfortunately, you will not be able to see him."

"I greet you all. I am sensing a presence inside the walls of this mastaba. There is a barrier of stone which greets those foolish enough to attempt entry into the funereal site. I believe your enemy and mine has reached that point. There are warnings etched into the rocks. I assume he has someone with him who can read the ancient language."

Major Akil spoke up. "I greet you, Lady Raamjet. I am Major Akil of the Egyptian Antiquities Police. It is our responsibility to protect the ancient sites and their contents. Until now, we had no knowledge of the whereabouts of King Tsk's tomb. In fact, most believed it didn't exist. It seems we were in error. In answer to your question, the mad Duck has with him a hyena who is highly skilled in the hieroglyphic writings of antiquity. If he has reached the barrier, he can read the warnings. What will they be told?"

"I am pleased to speak with you, Major. As you know, I am confined to the Underworld. That stone barrier is the point of nexus where the Underworld meets yours. Most tombs have similar obstacles. I cannot cross it but if the maddened Duck breaks through, he will be greeted by my powers and the vengeance of the gods who control the afterlife."

Octavius said, "We are here to keep him from breaking through. What lies beyond that wall?"

"There is an empty chamber where I keep watch. On my command, the walls and ceiling will collapse on any invader. Beyond is the King's burial chamber. Etched into the catafalque, bier and coffin are the instructions for his passage into the next world. His Book of the Dead. They were carried out faultily and he remains suspended between two states. It is my responsibility to see that he never makes the transition. The evil Duck must be prevented from attempting to bring him back to your universe."

"How can he do that? Does he have to work the spells in reverse?"

"No, just reciting the incantations as they are written will bring him back."

251

"I wonder if he knows that. What do you think, Major?"

"It's probable that Hyena knows it. I also doubt Imperius would enter into such a perilous venture without careful research."

"You're right about him. On the one hand, he is hopelessly headstrong but he is at his core, a very talented scientist. I have no doubt he has scoured the ancient sources to set up his scheme. Raamjet, you should know that the Duck has at his disposal one or more very powerful weapons designed to cut, blast and disintegrate any target, large or small. He used it to uncover this structure. He will no doubt use it to dismantle the wall. I remember you telling us that you are semi-immortal. What does that mean? Can you be slain?"

"Yes, but I am highly resistant to attack. In all the centuries I have existed, I have never had to test my mortality. I am also a formidable enemy."

"So is Imperius. Stay hidden from that weapon. Meanwhile, we are working out a plan of attack to keep him from the King."

"I sense his presence at the barrier. You may be able to conquer him while he is trying to bring down the wall."

"That is exactly what we plan to do. We shall speak again, hopefully after this is over."

"Yes, we shall. Farewell for the moment, Seeker of Justice and all my friends!"

# Chapter Forty Five

## *Inside <u>THE</u> Tomb*

*The whole anteroom's full of debris.*
*Are the three of them dead? Well, we'll see.*
*Could the villains survive?*
*Are they all still alive?*
*It seems very unlikely to me.*

Crackling sounds and the acrid smell of scorched masonry filled the anteroom and stairs leading to the barrier. Bigg Baboon was tracing the seams of the stones with the gun. With the ray set at a very fine aperture, the particle accelerator loosened the bonds that held the wall together. Succumbing to their own weight, the first few rocks fell from the top.

"Be careful, Baboon, we do not want the wall to fall on us." This from the Duck as he skittered back and forth, getting in the way of the projector and jumping up and down on the increasing pile of stones.

Hyena shouted over the noise, "We only need to make an opening big enough for us to fit through. You could probably fly into the hole right now, Imperius. Bigg and I will require a bit more space."

The Duck needed no further encouragement. Holding a high intensity lamp in one claw, he flapped his wings and soared into the darkness beyond the wall. "This room is large and empty. A twisted passageway leads out at the other end. Probably into the mummy's chamber. Hurry, Hyena. You must come in and be ready to find and read the Book of the Dead."

Hyena and Bigg looked at each other with a total lack of enthusiasm. The Baboon fired the weapon again, making the opening more accessible. "I think we can make it now. The radar cart will have to stay here outside the antechamber."

A skilled climber, the Baboon clambered up the pile of loosened material with a lamp in one paw and jumped. Once on the other side, he turned back to see Hyena still standing before the wall. "Pass me the ray gun, Hyena. We'll probably need it."

The Hyena stood transfixed. He was about to join these two idiots in a venture from which there might be no return. Not a very satisfying proposition. He shrugged, picked up the gun and climbing up on the pile passed it over to the waiting Baboon. Now it was his turn. Greed and curiosity got the better of him and he grabbed the last lamp and scuttled through the hole.

None of them had noticed a sinuous figure half hidden just outside the opposite side of the room. The Uraeus waited until the three of them were at the center of the chamber and then, flashing her glowing red eyes, she triggered the explosions that collapsed the ceiling and two of the walls. The intruders were buried in a pile of rubble.

\*\*\*\*\*

As Octavius and the team scaled up the side of the mastaba, they heard a roar echoing out of the opening in the roof. Massive clouds of dust gushed up and swirled around the surface.

The Colonel, who had reached the roof first, turned to the others and growled. "Well, there's one of two possibilities. Either Imperius and Bigg overdid blasting the barrier wall or they got through and Raamjet collapsed the empty room on top of them. Either way, I wouldn't give you odds on their survival."

Chita shook her head and said, "How many times have we counted him out. I want to see bodies as soon as this smoke and dust clears. Do we have any masks in the choppers?"

The Colonel thought for a moment and then shrugged. "Plenty back at the Ursa Major but none on board the copters." He turned to Octavius. "I think we'll just have to wait. By the way, I'm not sure you can fit in those passageways."

"I don't know. They got a hippo and his coffin down there." Octavius turned to Otto. "Do you think you can do one of your quick in and out routines and scout out the situation? Be careful! I don't want you getting hurt."

Neither did I. Talent agent Maury worrying about his client – Otto the Magnificent. Oh hell, I don't even have a contract with him. I just love the little guy.

Memories of falling down elevator shafts at Bearmoral Castle *(Book Three – The Case of Scotch)* ran through the otter's head. "Yeah, I think I can do it in short hops. Just give me few minutes."

Condo waved over at Octavius and said, "The Uraeus is back. She says she collapsed the room on top of them. They are buried under a pile of rubble."

"Well, that answers that question. Tell her to be careful approaching the debris. They may still be alive and may yet have their weapons."

Major Akil looked at Chief Inspector Bruce Wallaroo. "You're part of the international law enforcement community. Do you have any suggestions as to how we can legally proceed here? I don't think the government will believe a guardian snake did those three in. They won't even believe she exists. I'm still having trouble believing she exists. We'll need some kind of cover story. Accidental self-inflicted destruction by the raiders, perhaps."

Wallaroo spun around several times and blurted, "Major, I just want to see proof that our bloody nemesis is well and truly dead. I am damn tired of having him and his ape reappearing after we've counted them out. You can make up any story you want about the Hyena. Died helping tomb robbers. I don't think we want to spread the story that Imperius was trying to revive that rotten Pharaoh and his armies. Nobody would believe us. Let's keep the story short and sweet but first let's make sure that damn Duck is really dead.

"OK!" said Otto, "I'm ready. I need a light. I'll be right back."

And he was. Nobody, including him, knows how he does it.

"There is a huge pile of stone lying in the room. The barrier wall is down, too. I didn't hear anybody or see anything moving. It was silent as a tomb."

# Chapter Forty Six

## *Under the Wreckage*

*Bigg Baboon's days of living are through.*
*The conspirators now number two.*
*The Hyena and Duck*
*Keep on pushing their luck*
*They're deciding just what they should do.*

Movement! Groans! *(Otto was premature in his report.)* From under a stack of limestone blocks a black wing emerged. Then a second. The falling ceiling had formed a cave-like niche and Imperius was in it. Once again, he had won out against the odds. Once more he had survived. So had his lamp. Pulling himself upright, he looked about for his cohorts. "Baboon! Hyena! Are you alive? Where are you? We must not let this deter us from our destiny. Come out!"

From the corner of his eye, he spotted the tube of the ray gun projecting from under a pile of brick. Where the gun was, so must be the Baboon. He hobbled over to the spot. A foot protruded from the pile. A Baboon foot. Pushing, shoving, hauling as best he could, he uncovered more of the body. It was Bigg and Bigg was unquestionably dead. Cursing his own misfortune, the Duck picked up the ray gun and once again called out for Hyena. This time he got a response. From the anteroom. "I am here, Imperius. As I was coming through the barrier, I heard the ceiling and walls begin to

258

groan and I jumped back out. It seems the Baboon was not so lucky. I assume you are now going to abandon this cursed endeavor."

"Abandon!! Abandon!! When we are so close. Once again I have survived. I have outwitted the primitive defenses of the ancients. No, no! We are going forward. We are so close."

Waving the ray gun, he ranted on. "Surely I do not have to motivate you to continue." He fired the gun once in Hyena's general direction. "Chuckle!  Just testing to see if it's still working. A bit battered but functioning. I made these units to be extremely rugged."

The Hyena replied, "I assume you realize that without me to translate and interpret, you have no chance of invoking the Pharaoh's Book of the Dead."

Stalemate! The Duck, sensing his one advantage, took on a reasonable tone. *(A very difficult thing for him to do.)* Consider, my laughing friend, what great fortune we have in store. Consider the power awaiting us. Should we crawl back out of here defeated when we have the very cosmos almost in our hands? Consider how your expertise will be praised and trumpeted throughout our new universe. Do you really want to pass that up? Is not the fact that you survived this downfall of stone enough of a portent of your immortality...and mine? Come, on to the coffin and the King!"

While he was expounding, neither of them noticed the cobra watching and listening from the passageway beyond. She had unleashed the avalanche of stone and managed to kill one of the interlopers. Not the ones she wanted. The Duck still survived and more problematic, so did the Hyena. He it was

259

who could read the Book of the Dead and call forth the Pharaoh and his lion and crocodile army. Her first impulse was to directly attack with her spitting venom and blazing eyes but that gun gave her pause. She would call the Seeker of Justice and confer with him while these two gathered themselves together. It would take some time for them to reach the burial chamber and discover how the Book of the Dead was inscribed and distributed on the various artifacts. Time to plan a joint attack that would overpower the trespassers.

*****

Condo signaled to Octavius. "Raamjet is on again."

The Uraeus spoke in a whisper. "I brought down the anteroom walls and ceiling on the three intruders. The Ape is dead but the Duck and Hyena still live. The Duck has persuaded the Hyena to press forward on their evil mission. I am hesitant to attack them alone for they have that evil contraption, the ray gun. I do not fear for myself but we must achieve a successful defense. I am not sure if they can use it to kill or disable me. They both must be stopped and the odds increase greatly if they are approached from more than one side. Will you join me?"

Octavius responded. "We will be there momentarily. We also have the ray weapon, two in fact, and will pursue them into the burial chamber. Is it safe to move through the anteroom?"

"Yes, all of the destruction is over. You must climb over and around the wreckage but it is passable. How many are you?"

260

"There are eight of us. Certainly enough to stop them. Wait for our arrival."

He turned to the team and assigned one ray gun to the Colonel and the other to Bruce Wallaroo. Each member had a high powered lantern mounted on a helmet. The Major had his own conventional firearm. Otto, Chita and I, explorer Maury, each carried a thick metal rod. Condo was taken up with the portable com unit he was using to keep contact with Raamjet.

"Otto, make another sweep of that anteroom and wreckage before we go down there."

The Otter zapped out of sight and was back in about 45 seconds. "The Uraeus did a spectacular job of creating a cave-in. I saw Bigg, quite dead, buried under a pile of rock but there is no sign of Imperius, the Hyena or their ray gun. I looked down a set of pathways and I thought I saw a light moving along one of them. I did not see Raamjet. It looks like the dust and rock have settled but you, Octavius. may have a problem squeezing through the cave-in. I think we're good to go."

"OK, let's get down there. Maury and I will take up the rear. If necessary, we can blast away part of the fallen stones with the gun to get me through."

The Colonel growled. "That may not be a good idea. We may still have the element of surprise on our side. I don't think he knows we are even on the site."

Octavius snorted, "He will, shortly."

# Chapter Forty Seven

## *In the Burial Chamber*

*Well, the hippo's quite massive, of course*
*And his jaws wield a powerful force.*
*So we can't figure out*
*What the Greeks were about*
*When they named this huge beast, "River Horse."*

Under the watchful eye of the hidden Uraeus, Imperius and Hyena stumbled and blundered their way through the passages beyond the caved in anteroom. False turns, dead ends, collapsed walls conspired to slow their progress. The Duck's frustration level was at a new high and he cursed the ancients who had dared to keep him from his rightful destination. Hyena struggled along, holding the high powered lamp up to the walls, looking for any indication that they were on the right track.

Raamjet moved along behind, keeping sufficient distance to remain unseen. At one point she stopped and glided into an alcove. After several minutes she re-emerged with an amorphous object caught up in her coils.

The Duck let out a shout. "This is it! This is it! Hurry, Hyena. We must begin the revival process,"

They both held their lanterns high, revealing a gigantic gold catafalque, upon which rested an elaborately decorated bier. On top of this was a huge mummy case painted and engraved in the traditional fashion showing the features and bodily structure of an enormous hippopotamus...King Tsk VI, tyrant Pharaoh of ancient Egypt.

Hyena approached the funerary structure, shining his light on each segment. Then he walked around the chamber staring at the walls and finally, up at the ceiling. He turned back to the Duck, shaking his head. "There is something very strange here. There is nothing written on the walls and ceiling. The catafalque bears the King's identity with a few flowery allusions to his royalty and powerful persona. The only writing that has any resemblance to a Book of the Dead is inscribed on the bier and it is extremely short. Usually, the book is a long series of incantations, magical spells and spiritual formulas; exhortations to the Gods of the Underworld for his safe passage into the next life; protestations of his innocent existence here on Earth; and pleas that the judgement of his heart by the vengeful inhabitants of the Duat and Anubis would allow him free access to the afterworld with Ra. There are often four sections, culminating in his vindication and the right to live among the gods. The only section written here is intended to guide the King to the gates of the Underworld, period. That's as far as they went. It's almost as if they wanted to deliberately leave him stuck in a meta life forever."

"Exactly, exactly! They hated him and sought revenge. He's stuck and I propose to call him back since he cannot advance any further. Once his spirit returns, we will exploit him and his armies. You and I will have his eternal gratitude for having released him from his exile. You must recite the incantations of the first section, all the while calling for his release from the trap in which he is held. Begin!"

The Hyena held the light next to the bier and traced the hieroglyphs, reading them aloud. "Go, oh, Ba and Ka of the King and take on another life at the gates of the Underworld. Be brave and stalwart in your pursuit. Await the coming of Anubis and the time of judgement."

Imperius interrupted, "That's it! Recall his Ba *(his personality)* and Ka *(vital spark)* to reanimate his Akh *(spirit of life)* here in this world. That will restore him. Call on the elements that will remake the King."

Hyena improvised a spell of return and waited. Silence! Then a sudden wind arose in the chamber swirling dust and sand around the room. A vortex rose over the King's mummy case and enveloped it, moving faster and faster and screeching as it picked up speed. It seemed to be entering the sarcophagus through seams on the sides and top. It disappeared and the room returned to silence. Imperius fixed a rapt gaze on the mummy case. Hyena looked nervously around, no doubt working out an escape route

From out of the shadows, Raamjet appeared, spitting venom and flashing fire from her eyes. She was blocking the exit. In the darkness, only her eyes glowed. Hyena swept the area swiftly with his lamp and shouted to Imperius. "There's a snake here. I think it's a Uraeus, a guardian of the tomb." The Duck swung the ray gun toward the glowing eyes and fired. The red lights winked out. Hyena moved stealthily toward the snake and saw in the gloom a reptilian body uncoiled and stretched out. Imperius chortled, "So much for guardian cobras. She won't bother us again."

He turned back to the sarcophagus. A deafening sound boomed out from inside the coffin. The top crashed open and hurtled to the ground. A muffled voice roared, speaking in the language of the Egyptian ancients.

"He is back. Alive after a fashion. What is he saying, Hyena?"

"Between the curses, he wants the bandages removed and wants to know who summoned him back and how."

"Well, remove the wrappings!"

"I am not going near him."

"You must! I can now dispense with your assistance and will unless you assist me in every way."

"Need I remind you, Imperius, that you do not speak his language. May I also remind you that he is not very friendly."

"Approach him. I will fire a shot from the gun to calm him down, if necessary. Of course, I will not strike him."

The Hyena moved tentatively toward the remnants of the coffin and the massive figure partially revealed. He was *(is)* a huge specimen. Was there any wonder that he terrified all those about him.

"Greetings, Oh great Pharaoh. We have come to restore you to your rightful place on the throne of Egypt. Long has been your wait to join the gods. We are here to bring back your life, your power and your realm. Nay, not your former realm but the entire world, larger and more populated than

265

you can imagine. I am called Hyena and this black bird is called Imperius. It is he who has planned and executed your return."

While he was saying all this, he was carefully stripping away the wrappings binding the mummified King. As the Pharaoh's head emerged, his eyes glowed with an ominous stare. As soon as his mouth was free, he roared again at full volume, the sound echoing throughout the rooms and corridors of the mastaba. Clearly, the King had returned. Part of his plight had been the constant realization that he was caught in a vicious nexus from which he could not escape. Now at last he had been released and he would wreak unimaginable vengeance on those who had dared to imprison him.

But first, he must regain knowledge. The bird puzzled him. Ravens and other black birds were evil omens. Was this one an enemy? If so, why did he release the King from his bondage. After long centuries, his mind was not yet able to fully comprehend his situation and surroundings. Protection! Support! His underlings. He must summon the Leonine Legions *(Lions)* and the Pharaoh's Phalanx *(Crocodiles.)* He knew that they had perished in the Nile and had entered a separate part of the Underworld where they continued to exist. Could this Hyena know about such things?

Now he must transition to full physical existence. He was hungry! He would demand food and drink. He must dispose of the wrappings that were still binding him. He flailed and shook. The bird and hyena both backed away. The coffin fell in pieces, leaving the bier and catafalque intact. He tumbled onto the floor with a crash punctuated with thuds and grunts. The Hyena approached and pulled some more of the wrappings away and was almost decapitated by the shuddering of the hippo's massive leg. The King swiped at him. "Where are my lions and crocodiles? Bring them to me!"

266

Imperius looked at him with awe. This animal was huge and obviously vicious. His jaws and massive teeth were gigantic. Bringing him under control was going to be more difficult than he had supposed. If necessary, he could set the gun to stun rather than kill. Perhaps a few warning shots would suffice. At the moment, however, a standoff.

# The Development of Civilization Volume 5 Part 3

## The Gods and Goddesses of Ancient Egypt

### *(From "An Introduction to Faunapology" by Octavius Bear PhD.)*

*The Big Shock that altered our world dramatically, occurred about 100,000 years ago. It was not too long after that event that the rise of intelligence and sentience in the fauna of the world began to manifest itself. We have discussed this progression in many of the disquisitions included in these Casebooks. We have not spoken much about the development of religion, however.*

*Over time, even to present day, many forms of creeds and beliefs have developed to explain and justify otherwise unintelligible phenomena. Many of these religious tenets proclaim the existence of superior beings whose influences affect every aspect of animal life. Differences in dogmas have been the cause of innumerable conflicts in practically every age and location and among just about all self-aware species.*

*One persistent characteristic of these convictions is the strong assumption that these superior beings not only exist but are in contact with and even live among us. While some faiths see these god and goddesses as direct rulers of natural phenomena - weather, the seas, forests, the sky - to name a few, others believe these deities live apart in other worlds or alternate universes. These positions are not mutually exclusive.*

The animals of ancient Egypt believed in a complex hierarchy of supernatural entities whose makeup changed during different periods, usually influenced by the rulers of each era. Some Kings invoked monotheism while others, no doubt under the influences of priests dedicated to specific gods and goddesses, supported polytheism of different dimensions.

As a Bear of Science, I have maintained a skepticism about religion in general and polytheism in particular. However, there are certain singularities and portents that are difficult to ignore or explain. This is especially true of ancient Egypt.

In this, our most recent adventure leading up to the discovery of the mastaba of King Tsk VI, we have come face to face with strong evidence that alternate worlds exist populated by beings unlike us. For example, we have strong reason to believe that a realm called the Underworld hosts alien entities as well as the spirits of the terrestrial dead. It may also be that the Underworld is divided into blissful and tormenting domains, each containing spirits whose fate has been determined based on the character of that spirit's life here on earth. There may also be a third domain in which the soul is held in suspended animation, neither blessed or damned.

This Underworld concept appears and reappears in many cultures, civilizations and religions. Seldom, however does tangible evidence such as we have encountered here, manifest itself. In previous documents, we have developed evidence of alternate universes in which the population is much like ours. One major variant is the presence or absence of beings like Homo Sapiens. These universes seem to exist as parallel to our own, sharing many common characteristics and progressing in roughly equivalent manners. See

269

*Book Four of The Casebooks of Octavius Bear – The Lower Case - for one such example.*

*The Egyptian Underworld is different and seems to serve as a terminal location for terrestrial life overseen by an alien population. Whether we will be able to further explore this phenomenon is indeed an open question.*

# Chapter Forty Eight

## In the Passages of the Tomb

*As Hyena recited the spell,*
*Came a moment too dreadful to tell.*
*When the Pharaoh gave vent*
*All our senses were rent.*
*Like a visit from some kind of Hell*

Otto, the Colonel, Bruce and Chita led the way followed by the Major and Condo who was trying to keep the com channel open to Raamjet. Octavius and I took up the rear. Down through winding stairways and passages. Referring to the twins' game, Otto had scoped out the route on his previous run and we followed. We had just come upon the caved in anteroom when a massive roar echoed through the tomb. An animal roar! Condo was having no luck contacting the Uraeus. Our first surmise was probably correct. Imperius and Hyena had successfully reawakened the King and he was not taking it too kindly. Octavius needed some assistance working his way past the wreckage but with a little help from the Colonel and the ray gun, he made it through.

As they rounded a corner, they came upon the lifeless body of the Uraeus. "Oh gosh. Raamjet is dead."

A hiss and a whispering voice. "No, she is not. The Duck thinks he has killed me but he killed my skin. I shed it before I entered the room and in his rush to bring the Pharaoh back, he fired at it. He is a mad fool. I am waiting to see what the King decides to do. I suspect he will try to bring back his lions

271

and crocodiles. If he does, that will be the time to send them all back into the halfway world forever. I have contacted Anubis and he and the other gods of the Underworld are prepared to deal with them all."

Octavius smiled *(a rarity)* and said, "We are here to assist and to ensure Imperius and Hyena are not able to do any further damage."

In the next room, the Pharaoh bellowed once again. I looked at the snake. "What is he saying?"

"Small One, he is crying out for vengeance on those who imprisoned him and is summoning the Pharaoh's Phalanx and the Languishing Leonine Legions. The crocodiles and lions. He is completely ignoring the Duck which must be driving him madder than he already is. He speaks only with the Hyena who knows the ancient language."

There was a sudden silence and then a chorus of rumbles as the crocs of the Pharaoh's Phalanx swept into the next room. We stood in the darkened passage and watched as they surrounded the catafalque and bowed to the King. This was followed by another round of deafening roars. The Pharaoh acknowledged them and began a lengthy speech in the old language, broken sporadically by rumbles from the crocodiles. Clearly he was calling for them to rise up and reclaim that which was stolen from him and them. If there was a crocodile equivalent of a war cry, we were hearing it. None of us spoke.

Then a rhythmic, thumping sound echoed from the opposite chamber and far passage way. Tramping paws! The lions too, were answering the call of the King. It was difficult to tell how many there were. The line of march stretched well beyond our limited view. When the leaders reached the

272

catafalque, the entire procession broke out in a horrendous growl that echoed throughout the chambers and tunnels. The Pharaoh addressed them in what seemed to be a similar fashion. I looked at Raamjet who nodded her head. Same speech. By now the tomb and the outer rooms were overflowing with unlimited ferocity. The King's followers were angry and seeking revenge.

Imperius was caught within a group of crocodiles who either ignored him or sized him up and down as a potential snack. He was screaming and ranting in a language none of them understood, flapping his wings and waving the ray gun. Big mistake. One of the crocs wrenched the weapon from the Duck's claws and tossed it across the room in our direction. So far, none of the outraged mob had noticed us. That quickly changed. One of the lions peered into the shadows and sniffing loudly, advanced toward us. The Colonel fired off a shot that stopped the cat in its tracks. Snarling, he turned to the King and set off the alarm. Tsk VI was not pleased and ordered them to capture the offenders.

Chita grabbed the Duck's ray gun from the floor and with the Colonel and Bruce laid down an overlapping blanket of fire in front of the advancing horde. Raamjet unleashed an outpouring of venom and fire from her eyes and the Major was selectively squeezing off the bullets in his sidearm. Otto came up with an ingenious approach, zapping in and out of the oncoming mob and swiping their swords and spears. He tossed several of them toward us. Condo, Octavius and I had not been armed. *(Stupid of us!)* Now we were. Watching Octavius standing at his full height, brandishing a sword and roaring back at the lions was a sight worth remembering. Condo opened his wing span and with a spear in each talon staged an aerial attack on the now petrified crocs. Unfortunately, there wasn't a weapon my size that I could use.

As the melee was about to reach its climax, a deafening gong reverberated throughout the structure. Smoke poured out of every opening and fissure. Raamjet loudly hissed and shouted, "It is the god Anubis!"

A tall black jackal, standing erect, wearing an elaborate headdress and golden robes descended into the center of the tomb next to the catafalque. He pointed at the Pharaoh and in a resounding voice, declaimed in the ancient language. The King roared and then collapsed on the bier, falling on top of Hyena, breaking his back. He screamed for Imperius to help him but the bird was cowering near a wall trying to stay out of the jackal-god's sight. The lions and crocodiles fell back and slowly began to dissipate into the smoke and mist. The Pharaoh, too, gradually disintegrated, taking the Hyena with him.

As swiftly as he had appeared and disposed of the King and his minions, Anubis disappeared, leaving us, Raamjet and Imperius in the darkened shambles of the tomb. Octavius looked at the Uraeus and asked, "What did he say? What has happened?"

She looked up. If a cobra could smile, she did so and said, "He has condemned the King and his armies to a desolate world from which they can never return. They must roam there in constant torment and uproar. The Hyena was taken with them but there still remains here our major adversary, the Demonic Duck."

While she was speaking, Imperius had reached out and picked up one of the ray guns. Screaming his hatred for Octavius and all of us, he took the gun and aimed.

He was knocked over by a flash of light, then another and another until he no longer moved. Chita held the weapon at the ready and asked, "Is he dead? After he tried to do me in several times, I swore I would kill him and I did. But I'm sure you'll all agree. He was trying to kill us. It was self defense. Is he really dead? Finally?"

Otto and the Colonel both prodded at the lifeless body and shook their heads. Imperius Drake was no more. I patted Chita on the back. She sobbed or was it a sigh of relief? The Great Bear nodded at her with a mixture of sympathy and admiration...two gestures I would never have thought he'd extend to the cat. He turned to speak to Raamjet again but the Uraeus had disappeared. "Hmm!"

Octavius looked around at the wreckage and back at the body of the Duck. "Well, Major, how do we explain all this?"

# Epilogue

## *Back on the Ursa Major*

*We are now at the end of this book*
*And recalling the journey we took.*
*Yes, we traveled afar.*
*It was truly bizarre.*
*Just remember, the world nearly shook.*

Hugs all around. In spite of Mlle Woof's attempts to subdue them, the cubs were climbing all over Octavius and shouting. "Is the nasty Duck dead, Poppa? Is he really? He won't come back and try to hurt us, will he?"

"No, little ones. He won't be coming back. Neither will the Baboon or the Hyena. They are all gone."

Belinda was obviously relieved and grabbed the Great Bear's paw. Otto and I both gave Chita a high five which she did not return. Funny how you can hate someone but still regret that you caused their death.

Bruce and Condo were engaged with Frau Schuylkill, no doubt giving her a blow by blow or blast by blast description of the events.

The Colonel was supervising the return of the helicopters and drones to the fuselage of the C-5A with the help of the Flying Tigers.

276

Major Akil was on the phone to the Antiquities Commission, spinning a tale that could be believed and answering questions about the status of the tomb.

Octavius shambled over to him, said a few words and then shouted, "Listen everyone! The Major has given the Antiquities Commission a verbal report, no doubt to be soon followed by reams of paper and investigations. *(The Egyptian Mau shrugged his shoulders.)* This will be the official version and we will all stick to it."

The Major stared at the assembled group and said. "Based on confidential material given to us from an unidentified source *(Raamjet,)* we were informed of an attempt by an internationally known criminal and his assistants to uncover and rifle the tomb of King Tsk VI. Up until this moment, we were unconvinced of the existence of said tomb but indeed, the villains had managed to locate it. We don't know how. Given the limited resources of the Antiquities Police, I was pleased to accept an offer from Doctor Octavius Bear to use his extensive assets and personnel to foil their sacrilegious activities. The mastaba building was indeed entered by the desperados and we were able to pursue them inside the passages and tunnels leading to the funerary chamber. Along the way, they accidentally caused the collapse of the ceiling and walls of the anteroom, killing one of their number. The rest of them, upon reaching the tomb, committed the heinous crime of destroying the sarcophagus, coffin and mummy of the Pharaoh. Only the remains of the bier and catafalque remain. We do not know where or how they disposed of the King's body. During our attempts to forestall their acts of destruction, the mastermind, one Imperius Drake, was shot and killed. His body and the body of his assistant, a baboon will be transported to Cairo for further examination.

277

One of his assistants, Hyena by name, has disappeared. We are extremely grateful to Doctor Bear and his associates for their substantial assistance. We regret the loss of the King's mummy and the destruction that ensued. Further investigation will be forthcoming."

Octavius looked at each of us and said, "You have no doubt noticed there has been no mention of the Duck's real motives; the actual re-awakening of the King and his armies; the subsequent appearance of Anubis and his condemnation of them all, including Hyena, to a perpetual existence in an alternate world of terror and misery. You have no doubt also noticed that Raamjet, the Uraeus does not appear in the report. This is extremely important and you two, Arabella and McTavish, must never mention her again. She does not exist."

"But Poppa, she does too, exist. We were talking to her before you came back."

"Is this true, Frau Schuylkill?"

"Ja, Herr Octavius, she wished to talk with you on your return."

"Patch her in!"

We moved over to the screens on the cubs' play stations and waited while the Frau and Condo made adjustments. The cubs as usual were calling to the snake. "Come out, Raamjet! Poppa is here!"

Slowly a sinuous form emerged and once again, the glowing red eyes momentarily filled the screens. "I greet you all, Preservers of the Ancient

Lore. Anubis extends his gratitude to you for preventing the truly cursed King from arising. It is not known what evil he and his minions would have brought upon the world through the machinations of the malicious Duck. He is now in a place from which there is no escape. I especially thank you, O Seeker of Justice and your Lady Consort for your trust and belief in me. And especially you two young bearlets, my heralds and messengers. I shall never forget you."

Belinda asked, "Now that the Pharaoh is no longer in his tomb, what will become of you? You have nothing over which to stand guard."

"That is true, O perceptive Lady Ursine. I have been released from my burden and I shall soon travel across the sky in the sun ark and assume my place in the Universe as one of the gods. I have paused only to bid you all farewell."

Arabella sniffled and asked, "Will we ever see you again, Raamjet?"

"If you look up in the nighttime sky, little cubs, you will see my figure among the stars. I shall be looking after you as will all the Egyptian gods. And now I must depart. May Ra be always at your sides."

The screens went blank and so did all our expressions. The cubs ran to their mother. "Momma, she's gone!"

"Yes and we must never speak of her to anyone other than our little group. Raamjet and what has happened here must be our very deep secret. Do you promise?"

Reluctantly, the cubs nodded, "Yes Momma!"

279

Octavius turned to the rest of us and said, "And that same promise must hold for all of us.  If ever we required more proof of alternate universes, this episode seals it. But if this story goes public, the results may be catastrophic."

Inspector Wallaroo, who had been silent during the entire process spoke up. "I don't know how the rest of you feel but I am delighted to see the last of that Duck. One less character to drive me crazy."

Chita turned away. Frau Schuylkill growled and said, "Crazy is the word. He has been insane all these years from the first time he developed and took his verdammt serum."

Belinda shrugged and possessively grabbed Octavius' arm. "Perhaps it was the loss of his mate, Lee-Li-Li, that pushed him over the edge. And now, perhaps his spirit has been reunited with her. We'll never know, I guess."

Octavius simply muttered, "Hmmm!"


## The End of Volume Five of

## The Casebooks of Octavius Bear

# *The Curse of the Mummy's Case.*

# About the Author

Harry DeMaio is a *nom de plume* of Harry B. DeMaio, successful author of several books on Information Security and Business Networks as well as the five volume *Casebooks of Octavius Bear*. A retired business executive, consultant, information security specialist, former pilot and graduate school adjunct professor, he whiles away his time traveling and writing preposterous articles and stories.

He has appeared on many radio and TV shows and is an accomplished, frequent public speaker.

Former New York City natives, he and his extremely patient and helpful wife, Virginia, and their Bichon Frisé, Woof, live in Cincinnati (and several other parallel universes.) They have two sons, living in Scottsdale, Arizona and Cortlandt Manor, New York, both of whom are quite successful and quite normal, thus putting the lie to the theory that insanity is hereditary.

His e-mail is hdemaio@zoomtown.com

You can also find him on Facebook.

His website is www.octaviusbearslair.com

His books are available on Amazon, Barnes and Noble, directly from MX Publishing and at other fine bookstores.

# Also from MX Publishing

MX Publishing is the world's largest specialist Sherlock Holmes publisher, with over a hundred titles and fifty authors creating the latest in Sherlock Holmes fiction and non-fiction.

From traditional short stories and novels to travel guides and quiz books, MX Publishing caters to all Holmes fans.

The collection includes leading titles such as *Benedict Cumberbatch In Transition* and *The Norwood Author* which won the 2011 Howlett Award (Sherlock Holmes Book of the Year).

MX Publishing also has one of the largest communities of Holmes fans on Facebook with regular contributions from dozens of authors.

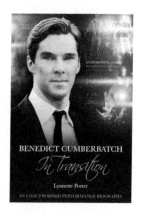

www.mxpublishing.com

# Also from MX Publishing

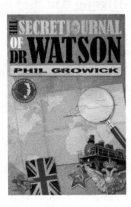

"Phil Growick's, 'The Secret Journal of Dr Watson', is an adventure which takes place in the latter part of Holmes and Watson's lives. They are entrusted by HM Government (although not officially) and the King no less to undertake a rescue mission to save the Romanovs, Russia's Royal family from a grisly end at the hand of the Bolsheviks. There is a wealth of detail in the story but not so much as would detract us from the enjoyment of the story. Espionage, counter-espionage, the ace of spies himself, double-agents, double-crossers...all these flit across the pages in a realistic and exciting way. All the characters are extremely well-drawn and Mr Growick, most importantly, does not falter with a very good ear for Holmesian dialogue indeed. Highly recommended. A five-star effort."

**The Baker Street Society**

www.mxpublishing.com

# Also from MX Publishing

## The Missing Authors Series

Sherlock Holmes and The Adventure of The Grinning Cat
Sherlock Holmes and The Nautilus Adventure
Sherlock Holmes and The Round Table Adventure

"Joseph Svec, III is brilliant in entwining two endearing and enduring classics of literature, blending the factual with the fantastical; the playful with the pensive; and the mischievous with the mysterious. We shall, all of us young and old, benefit with a cup of tea, a tranquil afternoon, and a copy of Sherlock Holmes, The Adventure of the Grinning Cat."
**Amador County Holmes Hounds Sherlockian Society**

www.mxpublishing.com

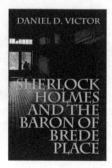

# Also from MX Publishing

## The Detective and The Woman Series

The Detective and The Woman
The Detective, The Woman and The Winking Tree
The Detective, The Woman and The Silent Hive


"The book is entertaining, puzzling and a lot of fun. I believe the author has hit on the only type of long-term relationship possible for Sherlock Holmes and Irene Adler. The details of the narrative only add force to the romantic defects we expect in both of them and their growth and development are truly marvelous to watch. This is not a love story. Instead, it is a coming-of-age tale starring two of our favorite characters."
**Philip K Jones**

www.mxpublishing.com

CPSIA information can be obtained
at www.ICGtesting.com
Printed in the USA
FFHW01n1732091018
48731975-52815FF